Send Me An Angel

Send Me An Angel

By ALICE NISBET

THE UNIVERSITY OF NORTH CAROLINA PRESS
Chapel Hill

To Mr. Ed, My Father

I'm feeling mighty poorly
Yes, mighty poorly,
I ain't got no strength, Lord,
I'm all trampled down,
So send me an angel
Just any old angel
To give me a robe, Lord,
And give me a crown.

From John Brown's Body
STEPHEN VINCENT BENET

ONE

It was the Christmas after the first flood in nineteen thirty-six that Delilah came to Mr. Ed's. It had been a hard fall, scant and cold, and would prove a harder winter. Most of the corn had been ruined, and several of the haystacks were washed away by the high waters. Mr. Ed had not counted on taking in more Negroes, but Delilah had put up such a poor mouth, and the Oggs whom she wished to leave were such shiftless poor whites, that he had promised against his better judgment to let her have Old Walner's cabin. He knew she was a lazy nigger; he had hired her by the day to pick cotton that fall and realized her worth. But the vacant cabin hurt his conscience, so he took her in.

She moved in Christmas Day. Mr. Ed sent two wagons over the creek for her things, but she had barely enough to fill one. She and her crazy little son, Sammy, came back in the empty one with the driver. It was a wretched day, full of a bitter mist. The roads were impassable but for the wagons, and the ruts cut deeply at the clay places, and mud sucked at the mules' feet and at the wheels.

In spite of this Delilah's heart was full of hope. Mr. Ed was a good man—and rich. He never let his niggers starve and go ragged. He had a good heart. Delilah knew these things, and all during the first miles of her journey home she was grateful. Afterwards she sometimes forgot.

Little Sammy said nothing before her on the wagon floor. He held to her skirt and leaned over the wagon side to watch the mud turn up with the wheel and follow it around. Occasionally it would be whirled off, sometimes hitting Sammy's face. He would grin then and lick his lips, eating the dirt from around his mouth.

The driver watched the little half-wit superciliously; he himself was young and strong and powerfully built with a mustache on his upper lip cut into by a whitish scar that marred his mouth when he laughed. But he was a handsome nigger, so godlike was his build. This companion, Pignine, and the hope that lay in Delilah's heart made her gay and inquisitive for a moment.

"Ain't you Miz Hannah's boy?" she asked.

"Yeah." Her companion's eyes left her son and looked far down the winding road that lay beyond the mule's flapping ears. He flipped the reins over their backs and absently clucked them up.

"You done forget me, I reckon," Delilah continued.

"No, I reckon you must be Cream Stewart's wife."

"Yeah, dat's me all right."

"Where Cream now?" Pignine asked pointedly.

"Lawd," Delilah pouted and gazed sulkily at the huge shoulders beside her. "How I know where he is? I ain't got no talk wid Cream Stewart."

"He yo' husband, ain't he?"

"My husband! Nigger, I may's well say you's my husband. I ain't been livin' wid dat Cream more'n two year now. I ain't never wantin' to see him no mo'! Huh, de way he treated me. My husband! You knows I ain't see nothin' of him."

"Well, dat's good. You better not see nothin' of him 'round dis place. We don't like Cream Stewart dis side de crick. He's a mean nigger."

"You can't tell me nothin' 'bout de meanness of dat nigger. Ain't I live with him off and on more'n ten year? Looky here, Nigger, I got a scar down my back two foots long he done put dere wid a nailed plank. And de way he acts wid other women— takin' up wid dat sassy young'n of William Foster's. Why, Boy, he uster take my own money and doll her up wid it, and she'd come sash-shaying by my house painted up like de devil, wid a hat on I know I done paid for. Well, I ain't standin' for no fool nigger actin' up like dat, so when he lef' me, I say, 'Good riddance.' And I ain't seen no mo' of him 'cept dat time he come back for Sammy. He love dat fool child more'n his own Paw would. Lawd, but he ain't gonna git him. No sir, if he takes Sammy, he takes me, and de bof of us is more'n he can handle."

Pignine looked down at the child who had turned at his mother's talk and was watching her intently and grinning. The grin cracked the mud on his face and wrinkled it.

"Jesus," Pignine thought. "It ain't much to love."

They had reached the creek now, and the cold mist turned into a heavy, slow drizzle. Delilah squeezed Sammy on the seat between herself and Pignine and covered him over with part of her coat. The three of them looked awkward and lonely in the gloomy landscape. They rode in silence for a while and watched the rain without interest.

At last Delilah asked, "Mr. Ed's a fine man, ain't he? He don't let his niggers want for nothin', do he?"

"Yeah, he all right."

He more'n jus' all right. How much cotton you got?"

"We got some cotton maybe, but we ain't got no corn. The river done got dat, and how a nigger gonna live without he got corn?"

"Well, he provides, don't he? You ain't starvin', is you?"

"No, we ain't starvin', but sometimes it's thin pro-vidin' we git. Look at de brick yard hands—what dey git a week, and work not half as hard as field hands."

"Yeah," Delilah said, remembering her husband. "Dey makes de money and dey spends it, too, easier'n any other niggers I knows of. Sometimes I hates dat brick yard."

"You got no mind to hate de brick yard, woman. You all lives off'n it, and de livin's right rare. You know, I think I'll work for dat brick yard someday. Gals likes a brick yard nigger."

"Huh, I's never liked 'em. Dey's too gen'rous wid dere temper and stingy wid dere faithfulness. De womens likes dem and dey likes de womens, and it ain't good for things to get too much dat way. Boy, iff'n you wants to be happy, you want to have one woman, and iff'n she ain't enough, you needs to be private-like wid de others. No woman dat's decent gonna stand the public knowing 'bout her man. It ain't de right thing."

Pignine laughed. "Yeah," he said. "You's a woman. But I's a man, and mens jus' don't see things dat way. Yeah, I think I'll work for de brick yard next spring."

Little Sammy had gone to sleep between them and Delilah shifted his weight restlessly against her shoulder. Life seemed suddenly cold to her and too endlessly long.

She sighed and said absently,

"Yeah, son, you go work for yo' brick yard and make yo' dough and have yo' sassy gals. It's an old black woman got no place 'round. Whut de white folks leaves, de black mens gits. She ain't got no chance."

TWO

It was almost dark when Pignine whoaed the mules on the beaten gray clay under the oaks that dwarfed Old Walner's cabin. The red mud of the big road lay in two narrow, crooked ribbons behind them and made a thick, sluggish mess among the gnarled roots where the mules stomped it restlessly as Delilah climbed from the wagon and Pignine handed little Sammy to her.

The cabin lay dim and huddled before them. The rain dripped from the blackened oak branches onto the ruffled shingles of its roof. The woods were behind it, and to the left stretched the red ploughed earth of cotton fields laced with purple stalks left from the summer's crop. The fields dwindled to flatness as they reached far to the pines that were misty now in the dampness. Smoke rose in spasmodic puffs from the piled rock chimney. Only the motion of it was gay, for it itself was as bleak and colorless as the sky above. But that smoke told of life in the cabin other than the ghosted life of Old Walner murdered by his wife's hand. It held promise for Delilah of warmth and cheerful giving.

"Maw must be here," Pignine said, holding the reins listlessly between his knees and peering up at the puffs of smoke. "She musta' 'done settled yo' furniture. De other wagon done been here and gone by de tracks."

Delilah made no talk but dragged her half-wakened son up on the unroofed stoop and then barged abruptly into the cabin.

Hannah sat before the hearth. The furniture was in order around her—the big bed cater-cornered by the fireplace, the little one in the opposite corner. The newly scrubbed floor steamed from the heat of a roaring pine fire. The one shutter by the fireplace had been opened in hopes of letting out the steaming dampness. Hannah sat with her back to the door, one arm across her chest, the elbow of the other resting on it as she picked her teeth with a black-gum twig. There was in the way she sat the uncompromising importance and awkwardness that said finally, "I's done done my duty. Right or wrong, I's done it."

"I'll go over dere," she had told Old Miss in the kitchen after dinner. "It ain't fittin' not to be fren'ly wid yo' neighbors when you is in hollerin' distance. 'Course, Miz Delilah gits talked 'bout heaps, and de things Miz Minnie say 'bout her do sound bad. But I knows dat Foster fam'ly Miz Minnie come out of. Dey say dat sister Lizzie of hers is wid Cream

Stewart in Winston right now. Miz Minnie got to make de pot look pretty black iff'n she wants de kettle to shine some. But dat ain't my bizness, and if Miz Delilah want to be fren'ly, it all right wid me, and iff'n she don't like other folks I know 'bout, dat is all right too. But I'll go over and see her settled. She new here, and it ain't right actin' up over what you hears."

So Hannah now sat solidly before the fire she had built, and to Delilah's tired eyes she looked good and definite as if there would never be any unknown or changing quality to her. Outside Pignine shouted to the mules, and the wagon creaked heavily as it turned around. Delilah closed the door, muffling the sound. She dragged her drowsy son over to the hearth.

"Evenin', Miz Hannah," she said.

Hannah did not offer her chair so Delilah sat on the floor with her son's head on her lap. The other woman looked at him.

"He still queer-like?" she asked.

"Yeah," Delilah sighed, "He ain't gonna have no sense."

They were silent then until Hannah threw her toothbrush twig into the fire and settled comfortably for conversation.

"You couldn' of picked a worser day for movin'," she said, stretching her feet toward the fire. "It gittin' colder all de time. Lawd-a-mercy, I hope it don't snow wid de chaps all bangin' in and out makin' fuss over Santy Claus."

Delilah said nothing. Little Sammy was again asleep, his twig of a body stretched along the ashy hearth. His mother moved him further from the blaze.

"How long dem Fosters been here?" she asked with hesitant aggressiveness.

"Miz Minnie?" Hannah turned to her. "Dey come wid me, goin' on two year now."

"I never knowed dey was here. Me and dem Fosters don't git along."

Hannah rubbed her cheek, and a sly smile spread over her face. "You ain't de onliest one I know dat don't get along wid dem Fosters. Dey's Baptist, and 'course I don't have nothin' 'gainst Baptist pertic'lar, but dem Fosters thinks dere religion de all-sanctified way; and Miz Minnie and Mr. Joe dey simper 'round and go to church liken' it wouldn' be none if dey warn't dere. Well, I ain't Baptist, but if de Lawd wants to burn me for dat, I'll burn, but I don't see dat it's any of dere bizness. I ain't never heard of a Baptist neither dat talked wid de Lawd pers'nal and He told him bein' Baptist shore was de only way to heaven. I say it's de deeds you do dat counts wid de Lawd, and dey don't seem no better over dere dan me. Dey hides as much meanness as me, and dey don't act as Christian sometime in my way of thinkin'. But hit suit me fine for dem to set on dere front porch and me to set on mine and us's to look at each other dat way.

"Dey ain't even needin' to look at me," Delilah said slowly, "and dat Minnie better not ever look at me. I knows what she say 'bout me 'hind my back. She needn't bake on both sides front of me. I know her and dat Lizzie sister of her'n."

"And dat Carrie!" Hannah said triumphantly. "Dat Carrie of Minnie's—she jus' like 'em. Think herself so fine. Think herself so mighty fine. But time'll tell pretty soon how fine she is. Time'll tell she jus' like de rest of us and no better'n my Totsy."

Hannah turned to Delilah and gave her a long look full of meaning.

"Carrie is sick," she said.

"How sick?" Delilah asked without much interest.

"Jus' sick. Like other folks. In no diff'unt way. But she make you think it diff'unt. She tell her Maw how a sickness come on her down at de river. Down at de river," Hannah scoffed. "And den she got her Maw worrit mighty nigh to death over her faintin' spells and nothin' settin' on her stomick."

Delilah looked up at Hannah, but meeting the half-smiling profile of the other's face, she only sighed and looked down at her sleeping son and stroked his kinky head.

"Mr. Joe," Hannah went on, smacking her lips

over her subject, "he come over to my house and say in dat high little voice he got, he say, 'Sister sick', and I say, 'Dat so?' and he say, 'She got a sickness,' and I say, 'Dat too bad, who done got her in trouble?' Den he prance 'round real straight and get all heat up and say, 'Ain't nobody touchin' my gal! If she done dat she know she never be 'lowed to come in my house no mo'! No,' he say, 'it ain't dat. Hit's jus' a sickness frettin' her. No, my Carrie's a good gal. She stay home where she belong.' And I know he aimin' at my Totsy, but Totsy a growed gal, and at least she never lied to her Maw. So I says Carrie wors'n her, and you just wait, time'll bear me out."

Delilah said nothing. A sort of hurt lay within her, and she felt little of Hannah's triumph. She did not know Minnie's Carrie, except that she was a thin young thing with a winsome smile and a switching way that reminded her of herself at that age. However much Delilah hated that family, it was somehow sad that youth should grow old and be sinful after all. Things were never the way they were talked anyway; Hannah could smack her lips over the weakness of Carrie, but Delilah knew that out of weakness and sin things sometimes grew dearer than out of goodness. The child on her knee was not Cream's child but was born of pure passion, ugly and twisted of mind. Yet in that little black life coming from sin lay all Delilah's love and hope and joy. The best and sweetest of all her happiness had grown from that sin. While Cream, her lawful husband, whom she had loved discreetly as well as passionately, had brought her misery and heartbreak and hate. No, there was little you could say about some things for what you said was never right. Drearily then, Delilah filled the silence with other words.

"Pignine done told me he goin' to de brick yard come spring."

Hannah's thoughts were shattered, her triumph, too.

"Yeah," she said. "Pignine like his Paw, and his Paw was a man all over hisself. Mens never knows when dey is well off. Mens is never sat'sfied."

Hannah was depressed now. Pignine was her first-born son and dear to her heart. He filled her heart with pride in his gay, masterful ways; but he broke her heart, too, for those same reasons. The reminder of his willfulness killed her exultation. She rose.

"Well, Miz 'Lilah," she said. "I'll git on home. I done what I could wid de house, po' as it is, and I's close 'nuff to you to help out however I can. Jus' call on me."

Delilah did not rise for fear of waking Sammy.

"Goodbye, Miz Hannah," she said.

Hannah was already at the door, and in the thudding of the rain drumming on the rotting shingles of the cabin roof, she hardly heard the goodbye.

"It look all right, de furniture," Delilah was continuing.

Hannah paused and stuck her head back through the door before closing it, expecting more to come. Delilah was still sitting as she had been before the fire, her head turned to the opened window where the wet trunks of the old oaks were blurred by the cold mist of the rain, where the chicken coops huddled sluggishly as if they melted in the dampness.

Hannah shook her head on the dreary figure and shut the door. She did not hear the last words of Delilah's thanks.

"I's glad you come," Delilah said to the closed door. And then again turning to the sparkling fire, "I's glad you come, Miz Hannah."

THREE

DELILAH was soon a part of the Big House doings.
Mr. Ed demanded not so much more of her than had
her last master, but rather that what she did should be
better done. She had often washed for her white folks
and done huge family ironings with rusty flat irons
and milked as many as five cows; but never had she
been called upon to do things with order and se-
quence.

Hannah understood her incapacity better than Mr.
Ed or Old Miss.

"She jus' a nigger," she told them. "You make her
do, and she'll do. She is sorta like a chap. She never
been called on to do, but she will when she hafta."

So the master and mistress were hard and demanding, and Delilah was impudent and sullen. She rolled
her green eyes to Old Miss threateningly. She
humbled herself to Mr. Ed and from his lectures
grew into a better hand but never a joyous one.

But she was not unhappy in her new home. In
many ways her life here was easier and less bitter
than at the Oggs. Little Sammy was far gayer and
seemed a little more sensible, a little less pathetic

than before. He stood always hard against Delilah's heart, harder it seemed to her than he had those last months when she had carried him physically there, turning and pushing at her body. But she would not have had him not there, and if ever he slipped from his place near her to spend the evening with Minnie's children or to be absent from her in the fields, some part of her seemed cut away. A fear would swell from somewhere deep within her, and she would pray and bargain with God for his safe return.

"Let 'im come home safe, please, Lawd, please. Don't let nothin' happen to my little son. I'll be good, I swear 'fore Christ, I'll be good, if my son'll come home safe."

And Sammy did come home safe to his Maw. Always he came in to her and pushed his kinky head against her heart and grinned at her whispering, "Maw, Maw." And always he brought peace to Delilah's misery, and at such times she would think there was no other thing necessary to her living. He kept her life together. He brought order to it and meaning. He chopped her wood and made her fires. He swept the dust from under the creaking, bumpy beds. He fried the fat back on the big range in the lean-to kitchen. He put on the corn bread and took it off just when it was golden enough and edged with a crunchy brown. He went with her to milk the burnt-sugar jerseys of Mr. Ed, and he rubbed them in the hollow between their horns as they muzzled in the seed meal and tossed their heads when Delilah pulled at their soft udders. He asked nothing of Delilah. He loved her without question as easily when she was drunk and cursed him as when she showered him with kisses and wept over his imbecility.

The happiness of Sammy alone did not make Delilah's life better, but Hannah, too, brought comfort and understanding to her bitterness. When Delilah mumbled at Old Miss, Hannah would spit and say quietly, "She good to you, Miz 'Lilah. She good to you as she know how."

And the words, in spite of the rebuke in them, left Delilah calm.

Hannah was often in the cabin that first winter. She would do quilt-patching before Delilah's fire, and the two women would talk together when they wished, or else they would be silent in their separate thoughts. They judged each other tolerantly and allowed a deep margin for each other's humanness. They had no secret meannesses to hide; they had no shame before one another.

It was thus in the stillness of a heavy March twilight that Hannah told of a new trouble that had come to her. They had been silent all afternoon—Delilah sitting lazy before the fire, Hannah bent over the quilting frame. In the light their faces showed up bronze. Delilah's was round and dreamy, while Hannah's hollow cheeks worked with her inward thoughts. Suddenly she left her needle laced in bating and looked up at Delilah, her brown eyes somehow sheepish in their sadness.

"You been hearing things 'bout my house?" she asked.

"Yo' house?" Delilah came from her own world slowly.

"Yeah. You heared anything?"

"Who'd I hear anything from?"

"You ain't needin' to hear what I's talkin' 'bout from no one. You could pick it out de air it goin' on so thick 'round here".

"I ain't heared." Delilah said.

There was a long silence. Hannah went on with her quilting. Then she said in a low voice, "Pignine done gone to de brick yard."

"He been aimin' on goin', ain't he?"

And after a long pause, Hannah continued, "Carrie really sick."

"She been sick ever since I been here."

"Mr. Joe done gone down to see Mr. Ed."

"He go dere lot, don't he, to show he sump'n special?"

"Mr. Ed done sent for Pignine."

"You said yo'self he oughtn' to let him go."

"He done took Pignine and Carrie to Lancaster. Dey married by now."

Delilah turned around slowly in her chair. She looked for a long time at Hannah's lowered face and at the hands going so rapidly across the quilt. Her body jerked slightly.

"I'd kill dat low-down Carrie gal." She whispered huskily. "I'd kill her. I'd kill her, 'fore de Lawd, 'fore I'd let a son of mine bring her home to my house."

Hannah sighed deeply at these words and sat back in her chair to gaze thoughtfully at the fire, saying sadly,

"Hit ain't Carrie's fault. Not all tol', it ain't."

"Ain't it do'? How come you say it ain't? She a low-down, gigglin', sneakin' gal like dat Lizzie. She made Pignine do dat out of spite to you. She and her Maw together done dat."

"And what if dey did?" Hannah asked wearily. "Hit done now, and nothin' I can say can undone it. Hit done and finished wid."

"Hit ain't finished wid," Delilah said vehemently. "I wouldn' let it be finished wid. I'd kill dat gal 'fore I'd have her marrit to my son."

"Miz 'Lilah," Hannah said wearily, "I ain't killin' nobody. Whut done am done, and it ain't no more Carrie's fault dan it am Pignine's fault. Pignine, he a man, and Carrie, she a long-legged little gal, and what happened always do happen in dem circ'stances. It ain't nothin' nobody can do lessen dey changes Pignine into a woman, or else dey makes Carrie into a man."

"I'll kill 'er. I ain't skeared of killin' 'er." Delilah was working herself into a rage at youth and Carrie with the Foster blood, a sort of rage, too, at Hannah who accepted this thing and a deeper rage at Pignine whose happy thoughtlessness brought such hurt to his mother.

"I ain't seein' you killin' nobody," Hannah was saying softly. "You ain't even killin' Lizzie yet, who done stole yo' husband. How come you called on to kill Carrie, who done stole my boy?"

Delilah looked then at Hannah who was picking her teeth placidly, and the rage ran out of her and left her tired,

"No," she said slowly. "I ain't kill Lizzie. But let 'er come close t' me again—let her come close—and it ain't no tellin' what someday I might do to her."

FOUR

Soon March was gone, and the spring rains passed.
The days grew long and tiredly hot. It seemed to
Delilah that she had never lived except at Mr. Ed's,
and she loved it there. Many times a warm surge of
happiness would come over her as she talked with
Hannah or watched her son catching lightning bugs
in the cool twilight under the oak trees. Then again
sometimes she would think of Cream and of her past
life that had been so full of living, and she would
hate herself and all the world for the dullness of her
life now.

She missed Cream. Always during the summer she
had missed him more than at any other time. She did
not want to miss him and held herself above it and
pretended that she didn't. But had she confessed what
usually lay in her heart, it would have been that she
missed Cream. She did not miss him when Hannah
was there mumbling out her philosophies sturdily, or
with Sammy, but during the bright mornings when
she was so much alone, her whole self ached for him
and most especially for the things he used to tell her
of his thoughts and the lies he used to tell her of his

love. But she never acknowledged missing him, so no one knew—she least of all.

Pignine and Carrie did not stay long with Hannah after the baby was born, and Delilah for a while was too full of Hannah's loneliness to brood much over her own. For though there had been a stifled bitterness in Hannah's heart at the thought of her son's bringing his wife to her, there was a deeper and sadder ache at his taking her away. Hannah did not like Carrie. In her heart she hated her, but she saw that there was little in her son's wife to hate and that it was Pignine's love of Carrie alone that put the hate within her. She bit it back and held checked unnecessarily cruel words so long that in the end she said nothing. Whole days would pass without her saying one word to her daughter-in-law. Carrie sensed the meaning of Hannah's silence, and between the two of them a sort of understanding lay jealously unconfessed. Sometimes her husband's love, coming always before that he felt for his Maw, sang within Carrie a golden and triumphant song; sometimes it hurt her a little to see Hannah turn wearily from their tenderness to let her anger fly out to the younger children—the round-eyed Jesse, the Freda cut by God like a ginger cookie in her Maw's own pattern.

But in reality, it hurt Hannah more, their leaving for the brick yard than had their coming in the first place. And because of the contradictory ache Delilah felt in her own heart for Cream, she could understand more easily this ache now in Hannah's heart for this son who loved his little wife so well.

Hannah grew ill, too, after Pignine left and seemed sick at heart and lifeless. She was getting old, and she felt her body wearing out and growing incapable of doing the work required of her. But she would not give up. She felt in her bones that, if ever she once got down, she would never get up to the easy housekeeping of the whitefolks. And this persistence in her Delilah had no way of understanding, so that as they grew closer in friendship, in many other ways they drew further apart.

In May, one Monday as they sat resting over their dinner before Hannah took up her dishwashing and Delilah went back to her washboards, Hannah said, dribbling her corn bread in the pot-liquor of the greens. "I'd be all right if I could jus' git rid of dis pain here 'cross my stomick. It ain't so bad some days, and if I kin just keep goin' dose days it do git a holt, I'll be all right."

Delilah had no answer for her and little sympathy. She ate her greens a moment in silence, and after Hannah had sighed and gone beyond these thoughts, she said,

"Dey works you too hard here."

"I don't work hard as Old Miss."

"She ain't sick."

"It ain't her job either like hit's mine, and she don't git paid for it like I do."

"It ain't much pay you gittin'."

"It ain't much work I's doin'. It ain't nothin' to what I has done for lessen I's gittin' now."

"Dey gits more on de relief doin' nothin' dan we gits here workin' like we do."

Hannah looked at her.

"Nigger's ain't proudful like dey uster be," she said gruffly, "settin' on de relief drawin' a livin' for nothin'! You know dat ain't right, Miz 'Lilah. A nigger better off workin' anyway. My old man uster always be de easiest to live wid durin' de hard season when he come home so tired it ain't worth fussin' 'bout. Niggers is like dat. It don't do for dem to lay 'round and git fat."

"Huh," Delilah mumbled, drooping her own plump shoulders, "ain't nobody gettin' fat dat I sees of."

But she let the subject drop and smacked her corn bread without further words. Why was it she could never say the things she knew to be true? Hannah, as well as any one else, matched her word for word and twisted all her thoughts awry. But in her secret heart Delilah clung to them as they were and did nothing to soothe the bitterness that grew from them. She hated people, really, black and white. Even Hannah sometimes for seeming so stupid and unwilling to share her hatreds. Even Sammy on rare occasions for being born a helpless fool. And always God for the life He had given her. But never had she let her thoughts crystalize this last emotion, for God, she knew, would strike her dead for such blasphemy.

Hannah rose wearily and began scraping the dishes with her fingers.

"You better git on wid dat wash," she warned, "or de rain'll catch dem clothes."

Delilah rose, too, and left the kitchen without words.

Down behind the hedge under the locust trees, she dipped the clothes in water, mumbling to herself. She dragged them all out again after a half-hearted rubbing. Water splattered as she wrung them. Her black hands with their dimpled, sandy-colored palms twisted around the twisted clothes. She flung them to one side in a pile and leaned against the tubs, clasping their curved tin edges in her hands.

"Oh, God," her unformed thoughts whispered, "why is I here, a nigger, washing white men's clothes?"

FIVE

JUNE was hot upon the little drooping umbrellas of cotton. Heat waves rose, twisting the tiny stalks into rumbas, and the earth from which they rose danced too. Little Sammy did not see the heat waves rising, nor did he feel the sultry air about him; only a senseless contentment filled him as he chopped the cotton —cleanly, beautifully, bunches of stalks every hoe space, and no grass anywhere.

Up and down the long rows the black dot moved. The sun moved. The shadows moved. Down at the foot of the hill where the young pines grew thick, a bobwhite called; and the hoe in its rhythmic movement made a scraping sound. Motion and stillness, sound yet no sound, while high above the Catawba in one of Mr. Ed's fields, Delilah's simple-minded boy chopped his Maw's cotton, waiting for the sun to suspend itself high in heaven. Then when he stood still his feet would be planted in the middle of the little round shadow of his head, his toes sticking out and wriggling in the hot sand. That would be high noon and time for eatin'.

Miraculously then, he saw his feet shadowed almost before any time at all had passed. He left his hoe in the furrow and struck out across the field. He reached the big road and trudged homeward, looking at his feet, fascinated that they moved back and forth so faithfully.

Down the hill to the branch the shade was cool and thick. A woodsy smell was everywhere, and the water slushed along lazily beneath the bridge. The spindly legs moved back and forth, the toes pushed forward, the daddy toe sticking out further than all the rest. That big toe puzzled Sammy. His Maw had told him it was pappy to all the rest, but Sammy could not understand, then, why his Maw was not his pappy, she being the biggest thing in his life. When he had asked her who his pappy was, Delilah had remained silent. Little Sammy could not have known this was a subject sacred to her most secret heart. Of all her lovers, that one alone had Delilah's prayers and blessings.

Into Sammy's line of vision, between where his left foot was and where his right foot soon would be, a caterpillar moved, a round fuzzy caterpillar with horns and a green body plowed in furrows around the middle. Sammy drew back his right foot; he put it by his left and squatted beside the insect. She waved her horns and moved sedately on, down the shallow ditch and up high on the other side. Sammy followed her deep into the woods, slave to this charming life.

Delilah had come home wearily, too tired and hot even for feeling. The cabin beneath the oaks had looked cool to her as she dragged up the rooty ditch. The two tall cannas blooming almost under the door seemed cheerful. In the only window facing the road, an old chamber pot was precariously set, and long, lacy streams of parrot's feather hung from it. When Delilah unlocked her door, a swarm of young mosquitoes rose from the stagnant water that the plant loved. It was sweet to Delilah to enter the cool, dusty filth of her own smelly cabin. It was all hers to come home to, and there she could shut out all the world of black and white and be comforted.

She hurried through her dinner of fried cabbage and thin black-brown corn bread and set Sammy's back on the stove to keep warm. She bathed herself gingerly from a blue and white bowl and powdered her body heavily. By now she was in a gloriously cool state, full of life and enjoying living. There was a double burying staged for that afternoon and she was looking forward to the noise and emotion of the stirring event.

But little Sammy did not come home.

Fear mounted slowly within Delilah as she sat on her stoop and watched the cars hotfooting it to Macedonia Church. She was by turns exasperated and panicky. The heat was becoming fierce and it was growing alarmingly late. She rose mumbling and went to her back door and shading her eyes looked between the blue-touched cedars far beyond the withering cotton field. There was a clear expanse of earth and sky. She walked out into the hot sun and cupped her hands and called for Sammy. The echoes faded away, and the same burning stillness settled over the world. Sounds grew less from the crowd of wagons and cars as the afternoon wore on, and when, much later, Hannah's crowd stopped for her in the wagon, she waved them impatiently on. Young Tom and Jake would have to be laid in their sinful graves without her prayers and lamentations.

Delilah did not go immediately across the fields in quest of her son but went first down the cedar-and-locust-lined path to her barn. The whole little loft shook with her weight as she armed herself with a pitch fork. Then she descended swiftly and resolutely to the river bottoms. Had the Catawba stood between herself and her son, it would have parted as the Dead Sea, but of its own accord. Delilah's mouth was firmly set; her green eyes searched each lane and thicket.

She entered the woods, going down the steep hill to the branch. Here she heard the screams that came from the woods and sounded like they came straight from hell. Delilah met the sound squarely and broke at a lope through the heavy underbrush.

"I's a-comin', Son. I's right dere in a secon'."

The yells grew louder as she added hers to the tumult. Across the fence in the pasture woods where the underbrush was less thick and the trees grew god-like, Delilah came upon her son. He was dancing madly at the foot of a giant white oak. His mouth hung open quivering with hysteria, and the round, black face was uncontrolled and puckered with rage. The little squint eyes were tightly shut. As he danced, he beat his fists against the tree and hugged and tried to shake the trunk. Not two inches above the drumming fists, the green caterpillar sat. She wrinkled her nose, the horns waved back and forth. She wondered at the unearthly noise.

Delilah stood and watched this scene, and then she crossed the fence carefully. She went up to Sammy and shook him with all her great strength.

"You fool. You crazy, fool, little, black idiot. You damned, senseless, crazy fool. Whut you down in dese woods for yellin' for a green bug? Why ain't you home? You crazy, fool nigger."

Sammy went limp in her arms, and shaking him was shaking just so much of unresisting nothing. It was no outlet for fear and fury. Then Delilah saw the caterpillar still in the same spot on the tree staring boldly and calmly at her and twitching her knobbed horns with her queenly air. And Delilah laid down her son and took up her pitchfork and rose to her full height, and stuck that caterpillar fair in the middle. It popped, and green fluid oozed out. Little Sammy opened his eyes now that stillness had come back to him. He saw his Maw's back, and beyond it, the tree trunk with the worm and the pitchfork through it. He broke into tumultuous, high giggles.

SIX

THERE was a time in August of that year that Delilah and her son went fishing. The pond, which Mr. Ed had built many years before, was forbidden the Negroes. But on those days when the family was not at home, the Negroes often enjoyed a swim or fishing in great droves. The children would strip themselves and dive and swim in the delightful water and chase sweet bugs to the indignation of the ducks. Mammies fished in great contentment along the shady banks and yelled warnings to their offspring. The younger girls went boat riding with their friend-boys who slapped their thighs and roared with hilarious laughter or made sly remarks when the girls reeled in the tipsy boat.

But Delilah was not often of these parties; neither was Sammy. They fished often enough, but usually in the river or sometimes in the pond at twilight. Delilah had a stubborn dislike for the members of her own sex, and they returned the feeling. Hannah was one of the few friends she had ever allowed herself, and only on rare occasions did they go off for pleasure together. Little Sammy seemed the only companion with whom Delilah could be happy for long. Delilah and Sammy walked to the pond under a blazing midday sun. It was wash day, but if a rain came up, the clothes would just have to get wet. Delilah intended to fish in the holy pond, with the holy fish poles, from the god-damned holy boat. She and her son with her.

Sammy loved it always—the oozing, squirming worms, the water lapping against his toes, the heat going up in visible waves from the pasture lands, the snake doctors weaving among the cattails. Today they caught a fish.

It was out in the middle of the lake after they threw in their lines that Sammy's cork began to dance frantically. He grinned all over himself when Delilah pulled out a perch, golden-bellied and shining. Sammy got down in the shallow water of the boat and held it captured. He fished no more that afternoon, but sat and stroked his fish, squeezing it still when it flapped. He giggled or stared in curious intentness at his trophy.

Delilah talked to Sammy all the time. She told him many things. How she was dirt under white folks feet, and they no better than she. How they made her work for nothing, and drove her when they wanted, and let her rest only when they wanted. How Mr. Ed fussed and threatened, and how God made them one and the same, except for color.

Sammy looked from his fish to her as she jerked her pole around. He stroked his fish and said nothing. Sometimes he smiled at his Maw and laid his black wool against her knees. At such times Delilah would turn her head and look far across the water. Then she would be silent and sigh in great, deep gasps, happiness coming over her in spite of herself, as she sat in the boat beneath the blazing sun against the cool water.

Much later the two of them went home. Sammy carried his fish on a pronged stick. Delilah went along slowly with her son. She sang loudly and beautifully; she looked out across the fields and through the woods. Her song filled her soul and body. She felt gay and at peace.

After dark, the milking done and supper over, she sent Sammy to Miz Hannah's and went to Van Wyck with Mr. Joe in his car. There she bought fish and walked up and down the street. Most often she went to the beer stand with some Negro man who bought her beer or wine. Later she begged bootlegged whiskey from the local moonshiner. By twelve o'clock she was gloriously drunk and loud-mouthed and very gay and restless. She backed friends into corners and confessed her sins and told her troubles. Sometimes she almost wept. Her eyes were a light greenish color, and they looked drowsy. She cursed Mr. Joe for leaving her, asked for other ways home. She left her fish in a ditch along with her supper. It was morning when she reached the farm, half dead.

Sammy had stayed all night with Miz Hannah, but he had missed his Maw and had slipped from the cabin at sunrise. He had gone home and sat on the door step for three hours till he saw Delilah dragging in. He ran to meet her, and she put her hands on his shoulders, and they floundered into the cabin together. Delilah fell across the bed and snored loudly until noon. Sammy cut some wood, he dug the garden, he sang spirituals in a high, quavering tenor. For dinner he sliced tomatoes and cooked corn bread. When twelve o'clock came, he woke his Maw. Delilah wept when she saw the pitiful dinner her son had prepared. She thought of the fish she had bought and lost and the money she had spent on liquor. She damned herself for the rest of the day and watched her busy little son with strange, sad eyes. For a week she was worthless to anyone.

SEVEN

ONE day in early October Delilah sent little Sammy to Old Miss for an onion to flavor her beloved vegetable soup. She busied herself in the kitchen until he should come back, for that was the most comfortable room in the house, being newer than the rest of the cabin and less likely to leak—it was delightfully warm and less smelly, or maybe more smelly, but with better smells. The cracks in the old iron Home Comfort sparkled in the duskiness of the rainy day. The burning wood sizzled and crackled. The kitchen shutter was open and Delilah could look out on her back yard jammed between the cabin and the woods. The chickens dusted themselves under the eaves of the house or climbed to their propped up keg nests in the cedars. The crib stood, grayed and old and skirted by shucks and wisps of dirty, twisted hay, and in the woods beyond the pigs grunted and slushed under the locusts, loving the weather.

The rain on the low roof cut out all sound save the potranck of Miz Minnie's guineas. Delilah did not hear the car drive up, or know that she was not alone until Cream stood in the door. She turned then, thinking it was her son, and faced her husband, grinning boldly at her.

She took in her breath sharply, "Oh, Jesus."

"Well, how's my old gal?"

Cream came into the room and threw his arms around her shoulders as if his three years' absence were merely a weekend.

"He want Sammy," Delilah thought.

"She ain't seein' you," she said, pulling away, feeling insecure but defiant yet.

"Whut you after, Cream? Iff'n hit's little Sammy, he ain't here."

"Sammy! Who wants dat half-wit? I wants my ole woman. I's lonesome for 'er." He rolled his eyes suggestively.

Delilah turned to her cooking.

"We done had dat out, Cream. You ain't havin' me, and you ain't havin' Sammy. You jus' may as well go on back de same way you come. Sammy ain't yourn, and I ain't yourn. And we's bof had 'nuff of you."

There were tears in her voice. This man had long been a habit to her heart, and it still cried out for him.

Cream remained good-natured. He came over to the stove and peered down into the pots. He raised the lid of the soup. It was bubbling exuberantly, turning and churning around with sun-scorched tomatoes. Steam and fat back smell came out of it. Cream smacked his lips and hugged his wife again.

"Ain't she always knowed what to give a man's stomick jus' when he wants it most? Ain't no cook like de one I got." He squeezed her close.

Delilah remained stiffly upright, the tin spoon held loosely in her hand. She tried not to give in. She knew her husband for what he was, but she had loved him in all her wild, gay youth when he had been one of a dozen lovers. She had loved him when he had been most cruel and despicable. Now, in her maturity, in her loneliness and weary misery, that love grew strong. Hate, too, grew with it. Yet knowing him made him no less dear. Now with his arm around her, flattering, warm, offering a little forgetfulness, she said nothing. Cream, holding her, looked around the cabin.

Sammy entered, shuffling and dirty and wizened. When Cream turned at his coming, and Sammy saw him there with Delilah, he withdrew forlornly into his bulky clothes and hugged the onion tightly against his chest. Cream grinned broadly and left Delilah and went over to the child.

"If it ain't little Sammy," he said.

Sammy stared at him, fascinated at his sleekness and his shining shoes; afraid yet of his strangeness and puzzling familiarity. He looked at his Maw and sidled around toward her. Cream reached for him and threw off the ragged cap and rubbed the kinky head.

"I got sump'n for you, Son," he said. His voice was gentle.

Delilah looked at the two of them. She leaned against the kitchen door and watched silently. Cream brought out a silver dollar from his pants pocket, and prizing open Sammy's tight-shut little fist, he exchanged it for the onion in his knotty hand.

"Dere's mo' where dat come from," he said.

So Cream sat down to dinner with his wife after three years. As far as he was concerned those years seemed never to have been. Delilah was only slightly heavier, less spry. And the man himself was unchanged except for his sleekness. Why he had come thus from the gayety and prosperity of his new life for a trembling, pitiful child, Delilah had no way of knowing. That he had come only for him and not for her, she knew too well. She who at all times was so hot to defend her child, now against Cream was defenseless. She was too used to being gay at his gayety, glad at his gladness to be herself in his presence. Sammy alone remained in his shell, unresponsive to Cream's affectionate approaches, staring solemnly at the two of them, listening to their talk.

The afternoon wore away as the early evening chill crept into the room. Cream told Delilah of his high living, of his fineness, of his importance. He watched her reactions carefully and hinted often at an enormous wealth. He flattered her slyly and was gay and rump-slapping. Delilah sat listlessly, half defensive, half responsive, altogether miserable and broken. When the cabin began to darken, she lit the smoky lamp and closed the shutter that the wind might not blow out the unprotected flame. She stirred the ashes on the hearth and burned a few pine knots to add more light to that of the feeble lamp. Cream lay on the bed and watched her and talked. Sammy sat at the foot of the mantel piece. When Delilah in her moving came near the bed, Cream reached out and pulled her down beside him; and she sat there stiff and still and listened to the unabating good humor of her husband's words.

In the evening, the rain stopped, and a wind rose, hustling clouds across a cold, brilliant moon. Cream got up and pulled Delilah toward the door.

"You ain't seen my car," he said. "It am a car."

He opened the door and coaxed his drowsy wife out, displaying the roadster at the foot of the bank. Its chrome glistened in the moonlight, and it made a long shadow across the sandy road.

"Paid seven hun'erd dollars for dat baby. Paid cash. Could'a paid mo', but dat car wuz de best bargain. Honey, you couldn' ever git another car like dat one for seven hun'erd dollars. De man I bought it from say Mr. Reynolds owned it 'fo' me and swap it in on 'count it bein' a bad 'bacco year, and he runnin' low on cash. Say he cried like a baby havin' to sell dat sweetheart."

Delilah looked, and a pride as strong as Lucifer's swelled her heart that a poor nigger she had married could scale the heights and own such a car as that. She left the stoop and lumbered out under the oaks and stared at it. She climbed down the embankment and went around to look. Cream followed her closely. He opened the door and took her arm.

"Git in, Honey," he whispered. "Let's give her a chance to show her stuff."

Delilah forgot her son in the cabin. She forgot the slyness of this man. She sank deep into the splendid blue upholstery.

"Let's go to Van Wyck," she said with a broad grin.

Cream slipped the car in gear, and they slid off in a gentle spatter of gravel.

Much later he brought her home, all the triumph gone. The bright glory of the evening was forgotten in a heavy drunkenness. Cream had great difficulty hauling her to the cabin door where Sammy met them sadly.

"She ain't to be woken, Son." Cream admonished him as if they shared some joke.

Sammy said nothing but helped carefully to put his Maw to bed. Cream, sitting wearily to catch his breath after depositing his burden, pulled the boy to him.

"Is you miss yo' Paw, chile?" he asked.

"I ain't got a Paw." Sammy would not look away from Delilah.

"Ain't it de Lawd's truf." Cream chuckled under his breath and then remonstrated strongly, "But dat ain't no way to talk. All boys got Paws. And I's aimin' on being' yo' Paw. I'll give you all de silva dollars you wants just to be yo' Paw."

"I ain't got a Paw. I's got a Maw."

"Yeah, Son, and look whut she give you. Is she ever give you silva dollars? Is she ever dressed you up in classy clothes and rid you in a sleek car? No, suh, she ain't, and she ain't likely to. But you jus' tie up wid yo' Paw here, and he'll show you de stuff. Son, how ole is you?

"I ain't ole."

"You is, too. Everybody ole, and you is 'bout thirteen by my calc'lation. Thirteen! Dat plenty ole 'nuff for a fine boy like you to be workin' and makin' silva dollars all yo' own. Wouldn' you like to work next yo' Paw and make money like him?"

"Pignine, he work and make money." Sammy wrinkled up his face and turned toward the man.

"Yeah, now Pignine, he a man. And Sammy, he almost a man, too. You jus' give him time and some work to do and let him make a little money."

Sammy said after some effort, "I ain't got sense to work."

"Ain't got sense? Go 'way, boy. You got plenty sense. Who say you ain't?"

"I ain't got sense to work."

Cream hugged him close.

"Want to ride in my car, Son?" he asked. "Want to go 'way and come home rich to yo' Maw?"

"Come home rich to my Maw?"

"My, won't his Maw be glad to see little Sammy all slicked up and rich. Won't she be happy?"

Sammy smiled faintly and turned and rubbed Delilah's limp arm.

Cream got up. "Now we got to ride in my car."

Sammy got up, too, and looked vacantly around the room.

"Dat's de man," Cream said and gently prodded him toward the door. He got him into the car which took all Sammy's attention until Cream started the engine.

"Where my Maw?" Sammy asked, his face wrinkling into stormy puzzlement. He tried to open the door, but Cream pulled him back.

"Be quiet, Son."

Sammy only whimpered as the car started forward in the early morning.

EIGHT

THE cabin was no longer whitened by autumn suns but staggered, gray and beaten, under wild skies. The oaks were bare above it, and in the restless winds they bent stiffly. Only the pines and cedars stood green in the distances, and the flattening furrows were a pale pink as if the winter rains had faded the earth. The hard bleakness of the winter froze even the adventuring heart, and most folks remained in doors, warming their hearths and viewing the wild elements with their backs to the blaze. It was a drunken winter. The days roared by in dark gloom or cold, bright sunshine. There were no deep snows, only driving winds and rains. Sleet, falling in the night, was hard frozen and impassable by morning. The older generation had not seen such times since their childhood.

It was a hard winter on the Negroes. They set rabbit boxes and consumed canned blackberries and corn liquor by the quarts. And to Delilah the winter was something awful. She needed the heavy heat of summer to warm her lazy bones. The winds caught her unprepared. The old papers were ripped from her cabin walls, and icy blasts whistled through it. Drafts darted all through the huddled rooms and screamed out only when others more fierce blew in.

Delilah allowed her mule to die from exposure, and because Sammy was no longer with her to need the milk, her heart was less than ever in the milking of the Big House cows. She squeezed their huge udders sparingly. The calves' tummies grew tight and full. Mr. Ed sent Delilah from the lot and turned the milking over to Hannah. And Delilah felt only bitterness at losing the job.

"Dey don't care nothin'," she mumbled. "I ain't got Sammy no mo', and dey don' care nothin'."

When she grew thirsty for buttermilk with her corn bread and sent one of Hannah's children to the house for some, the bucket came back filled a little over half with milk and overflowing with Old Miss's complaints.

"I would not keep her, Daddy," she would say to Mr. Ed. "The nasty, impudent old thing, sending here for milk when she could get all she wanted for a little honest labor. They won't do anything; they all expect to sit and be fed off the fat of the land. I would not keep her."

But Mr. Ed kept Delilah on. He had no heart to turn the poor, unloved thing from her one shelter. Without Sammy to comfort her and give cause to her work, he knew she had become worthless. But he kept her on. And Delilah had no thought of his not keeping her. She had no thought of anything these days but emptiness, the long stretch of life before her without any reason to it whatsoever. She never asked Mr. Ed to go for Sammy, and he did no more than inquire around for him, having found from experience that an outsider could make no happy solution to troubles between a colored wife and her husband. Delilah never thought of urging him to help in this; she never thought of it one way or the other, except that it was hopeless and that her son would never be returned to her. She felt too tired to bother, too tired to talk about it, to ask help of any kind. All she wanted in the world, it seemed to her, was to lie down in the night and never have to get up again.

But life was still in her, unkind and demanding. When times grew so hard as the winter roared past that fat back and lard, even corn bread grew scarce, Delilah felt the world had no right to starve her as well as take all the joy from her existence. She stole anything at all handy for food or money. Corn disappeared from the crib, and ribs and sausage rolls left the smoke house regularly. She sold the corn to white trash for almost nothing and bought fish, bologna, and her moonshine with the pennies acquired thus. She grew belligerent and shameless in her thefts and planned one night to take the whole of a small ham.

It was in the dark of the moon, a good time for stealing; and the night was cold and steady. The wind was still but Delilah's very breath seemed to freeze as, hooded and mysterious, she left the cabin. The road ahead of her was barely outlined, and the deep ruts that cut through it were frozen and un-yielding beneath her weight. Delilah was swift and silent in her wickedness. For a while, maybe, she for-got her Lord was watching. The night was very dark.

She hurried in her walking and rolled her eyes when the greyhound left her house and followed gently after her. Delilah passed the Big House and neared the wash-place. A brittle wind arose and caught up the ashes around the two black pots. It whistled, and a piece of paper flopped up with it. The crib doors creaked. In their stables the mules shifted restlessly.

"Oh, Lawd," Delilah said.

Her hands clutched at her throat, but her steps were still firm and silent.

The smoke house smelled musty and unaired but inviting, of hickory smoke and ashes, of hams tender under their hard skins, and of fat back damp and salted down. Delilah's watering mouth drowned her fear. She stuck her second and third fingers as she had so many times in the staple which held the lock. It pulled loose. The still rising wind whipped at her skirts. The chain rattled, the door swung open and Delilah went in quickly. She gasped and reached for the old scissors that were always on a high shelf just inside the door and were used to cut down the hams.

Delilah felt the trap then and drew back. But the spring flew loose, the steel closed, cutting into the bones of three of her fingers. She groaned, and in her awful haste and pain, she jerked at the caught hand. It broke away, leaving the three ends of black fingers bleeding in the trap.

Delilah did not show herself for a week. Mr. Ed burned the three finger ends in the house stove, and Miz Hannah reported as how Delilah had cut off her finger tips chopping wood.

When Delilah's hand became infected, Mr. Ed dressed it himself every two days. Nothing was ever said, but the bitter spot in Delilah's heart swelled, the loneliness of her life closed upon her; and the hams hung safe and sweet from their twine in the smoke-house.

NINE

Delilah woke in the freezing night. Her own mumbling in her dreams woke her, and she lay among her ragged quilts shivering with cold and fear.

"Oh, Jesus," she moaned.

Already the dream was forgotten, but little Sammy's face that had grinned at her amid its noise and confusion still lay behind her eyes and deep within her soul. It was bittersweet to have him always there within her but never to have him alive and warm in the flesh to feel and handle and love. She missed him more than she had ever missed Cream. With Sammy gone, she was merely existing because too much of her had gone with him to let her really live. Her days were a sort of hodge-podge of getting up and struggling around and going to bed and living in a shell of blank dolefulness—mind as well as body. So she lay now, frightened by the wind and cold and darkness, but only half conscious of it.

Then above the night noises she faintly heard hurried, shuffling, fantastic steps as if the wind blew leaves across the board floor. The old, rusty springs on Sammy's bed creaked just as if the weight of a small, young body had fallen suddenly upon them.

Bewildered with the night and the eery half darkness of the room, remembering vaguely the confusion of her dreaming, and seeing always her son's wrinkled, simple face, Delilah clutched the quilt edges at her throat and lay panicky still. Her heart beat wildly, sounding to her louder than the creaking clapboard and whistling wind. Fear lay within her—an awful fear that she had heard wrong, and an exultant fear that she had heard right.

"It ain't my little boy," she whispered. "You ain't sent him back, Lawd? Not to his sinful Maw? You taken him away, you ain't sent him back in de cold night to his lonely Maw?"

Her head lay buried deeply in the straw and covering. She was too afraid to look toward her son's bed. Too afraid that he might not be there.

Again the springs creaked, and as high as the wind, as moanful, as lost, Delilah heard—as she had heard a million times during winter nights—the voice of her son whimpering in the cold.

"Maw."

Delilah's bed contorted as she scrambled out. "Oh, Lawd Jesus Christ in heaven, You done sent me my son, my little nigger boy who ain't got no sense!"

The cabin shook under her weight as she stumbled across the floor. Loudly the wind howled, blowing to the Equator. It was not a night God would be merciful in. He made the elements on earth as wild as hell's lowest deep; fixed stars like burning, hating eyes in the cold, glazed sky; made His breath a mighty wind, and sweeping over all the earth, it warned the world of His vengeance.

But Delilah saw not all this. Only in the emptiness of his ragged bed, she saw her son's face, crinkling at her, tears still rolling on his cheeks, but his grief forgotten in his Maw's presence.

"He done come back," she whispered to the fates. "He done come back, grinning at his Maw."

All night long she sat beside the dirty, rumpled iron bed with its flaking, green enamel and agonizing design. She felt little of the boisterous cold of the night nor heard enough of its wild strangeness to be afraid. She knew no wonder at the return of her child, nor once doubted his being there in her trembling, exultant arms.

"He done come back. Oh, praise de Lawd Jesus, who done let 'im come back to me."

And Delilah wept anew and kissed her son now curled asleep in the straw ticking that had grown with his body and been molded by his shape.

"You didn' keep 'im away. Sinful as I is, You sent him back. My little son, my little son who ain't got no sense."

Toward dawn she slept deeply in her cramped position beside the bed and woke only in the high

bright noon with its gay, whipped wind and sunlight so bright and hard and sparkling that you could
touch it and feel it cold-hot like ice. She woke then
when the shutter came off one leather hinge and
banged against the chimney, singing a low broken
aria. Delilah rose, swaying and bent by her sleep, and
tied the shutter back with binder cord and made a
great hot fire that roared and snapped. She walked
grotesquely about on tiptoe, knocking chairs around
and falling against things, rolling her eyes toward her
sleeping son and holding her breath until she was
sure he did not awaken.

TEN

DELILAH was in the kitchen frying huge chunks
of Irish potatoes, standing far back from the stove so
that she could see her son's bed and him in it sleeping
like a child who knows himself secure.

Someone knocked loudly on the door to be heard
above the wind.

"Miz 'Lilah," Hannah called, shaking the door.
"Miz 'Lilah!"

Delilah went to the door quickly to hush the noise,
and the face she stuck through it was so rapturously
alive and full of peace that Hannah stepped back
from it alarmed.

"Whut ails you woman?" she said. "It twelve
'clock bright day, and you lock up like it midnight.
And den you bus' open de do' looking like you done
died and seed de Lawd."

"Come in, Miz Hannah," Delilah said huskily.
"Come in out de cold."

"Well, I ain't 'spectin' to stay out here all de day."

Hannah came in and went over to the fire, facing
it and bending over to warm her hands. Then she

turned around and held up her feet to the blaze one at a time.

"I come over to tell you Pignine comin' home. He been fired—"

The bright sunlight outside had cut her vision, and only now did she see the room clearly.

"Who dat you got in Sammy's bed?" she demanded, conscious of the sacrilege of anyone's being in Sammy's bed. "Somebody sick?" She peered hard into the dark corner. "Lawd Jesus," she almost screamed, "who dat?"

Delilah stood to one side between Hannah and the bed. She still held the fork used to stir her potatoes, and the odor of their burning was filling the cabin. But she did not move from her place, and her face was as raptuous as ever.

"Hit Sammy. Hit Sammy," she said, swallowing the words like people do who have not spoken sensibly for a long time.

"Sammy? Little Sammy? Good Lawd! Where de devil he come from? You know it ain't little Sammy."

"Last night. He come last night in de wind."

"Who fetch him? Did Cream fetch him home?"

"I ain't seed Cream. Sammy jus' come."

Hannah went over to the bed and looked down at the boy. "He awright?" she asked. "He real, ain't he?"

Hannah sighed and turned from the bed. "You got 'im back," she said pulling a chair up to the fire. "See you keep 'im here." She looked keenly at Delilah and shook her head dubiously.

The little room had filled with the acrid, choking smoke of fat back. Hannah noticed it first.

"Whut you burnin' up on de stove like dat? Sometimes you ain't got no mo' sense dan a chap. Standin' in de middle of de flo' wavin' a fork like a fool. Lettin' yo' meat burn to a little kink."

Delilah went into the kitchen, and Hannah talked on to her from her place by the fire.

"Pignine done left de brick yard. He fired. I told him when he tell de gov'ment men dey work him overtime, dey'd fire him for dat lie. He say dey couldn'. He say dem gov'ment men say hit agin de law. He know now whether dey can and dey can't. He fired now, and he comin' back to Mr. Ed. He and Carrie."

Delilah came to the door.

"Sammy woken?" she asked. "Don't you talk so loud and wake Sammy."

"He ain't woken. He sleep all dis day. Can't you see de way he sleepin', he mos' daid? He ain't nothin' but skin and bones. He ain't nothin' but a shell he so po' and tired. He'll sleep."

Delilah looked at him, and the joy left her face,

and she sighed. She had hardly noticed Sammy's thinness, but now the bones stuck out in his chest and arms in a startling fashion.

She sighed again. Her eyes saddened, and a vengeful, fearful look flitted over them.

"So Pignine bringin' Carrie to yo' house," she said.

"Hit awright, dey's comin'," Hannah said. "Hit all right. Hit ain't done Pignine no good being close to Van Wyck. He married now. He needin' to settle down; and dat Carrie, she ain't so bad. She been right patient when it ain't easy to be patient. She makin' as good a wife as any to be such a chap."

Delilah went over to Sammy's bed. She looked at her child and smiled as wistful a smile as Hannah had ever seen. She said nothing for a while but then answered absently, "Hit ain't Carrie you carin' 'bout. Hit's Pignine you wants back home."

Hannah gave her own sheepish grin.

"Yeah, hit Pignine I wants. He ain't steady like Jesse, and you can't lean on him none. But he like his Paw; he good to have 'round de house. He looks at things diff'unt. He laughs at 'em."

"Dere's dem dat laughs," Delilah said, coming over to the fire, "and dere's dem dat don't see nothin' funny to laugh 'bout. And it's mo' of dem dat don't 'round here."

"And you's 'mong 'em," Hannah said, grinning up at her friend. "Here you got Sammy back, and you already worrit over him lookin' so po'. And it uster be nothin' wouldn't ever matter if you jus' had him back."

Delilah sat down and looked at the fire, and there was something of fear in her eyes.

"Last night," she said, "when I see Sammy done come home to me, I's so glad I thanks Jesus. I say, 'I's a wickit nigger, but You done forgive me, and let Sammy come back to me.' And I say, 'I won't ever be wickit agin.' Den dis mornin' you come and say Sammy so po'. I ain't seed 'fore how po' Sammy is. But when I sees dat, I hates God. I hate Him 'cause I know He done sent Sammy to try me agin, and I knows I still wickit, and He ain't forget. And I's a nigger and dere ain't much chance His forgettin'. I done tried to be better, and I can't. And 'less I got Sammy I's de wickitnest nigger dere is. But to dem dat ain't got, de Lawd takes away. Dat's de truf. I knows it. I ain't learned it for nothin'. And I know He kin take Sammy 'way from me agin. He kin take Sammy," Delilah said as her voice rose and cracked. She cried with deep inward sobs that had little sound because they spent their passion within her heart. "He kin take Sammy, and dere ain't nothing I kin do. Dere ain't nothin'."

Hannah watched her with eyes that were watery and soft and shadowed. They seemed to float back and forth in their sockets. She clucked her tongue and, shaking her head, turned back toward the fire.

"Hit awright, Miz 'Lilah," she said. "Don't say nothin' like dat. You got Sammy now. De Lawd ain't takin' him away. He's dere asleep and happy. You be good to 'im. Feed 'im up and be good to 'im. De Lawd won't take him 'way."

Delilah was quiet again and comforted for awhile.

"I's tired bein' good," she said then. "I's tired. Whut I got to be good for? If I be good, maybe I keep Sammy, but how dat gonna help me none? I ain't sure I goin' to have him. Whut's dere for me so scared all de time? Why do de Lawd try me so? I ain't nothin' but a po' nigger. I ain't got nothin' but Sammy. Not nothin'. Why don't he try dem dat's got sumpin' to spare? Dey ain't no better'n me."

"Hit ain't no use talkin' like dat, Miz 'Lilah. Talkin' like dat never done nobody any good. Our lives ain't no mo' to de Lawd dan a day, and a day ain't much to nobody."

"Hit mo' dan a day to me. Hit's a long, long time to be in de dark."

"Hit seem like dat, I know. I been through it too. But dere's light sometimes, and dat's good. You got light right now. You got Sammy. You ought to be praising de Lawd, not talkin' dat way."

"Yeah. Yeah, I got Sammy. Hit's good to have him, I ain't meanin' nothin' wid my talk. I ain't meanin' nothin'."

Delilah was getting afraid. She knew she spoke blasphemy. After the anger was gone, she always grew humble and afraid.

"I got 'im. De Lawd good to send 'im back, and I ain't worth it. I know I ain't. I ain't meanin' nothin'. It jus' some things ain't bearin' laughin' at. It seems I can't never be happy no mo', nor laugh at nothin'."

ELEVEN

Spring came early. It was at first a lazy, subtle spring filled with high-sailing clouds and bright sunshine. The Negroes broke the soil and turned and mixed and fluffed it up for corn and cotton planting. Mr. Ed was anxious to get the seeds in early, fearing that such a spring would be followed by a dry, short summer. The early season was pushed almost too much, for some of the upland cotton was caught by unexpected frosts and had to be replanted. But such cases were rare, so that by late May, the corn and cotton fields looked especially promising.

Little Sammy followed the plow for the first time that spring. Not that the winter away had strengthened him any but because he wanted so to do the work and exulted so in the added importance it gave him. Mr. Ed gave him the big one-eyed, white horse, Dan, and the boy looked charming and pathetic and wholly inadequate, holding the v-shaped plow in the red earth and hurrying along behind it. His master was especially fond of the little half-wit and glad that he should do the work in his careful, patient way. The other hands, shamed that such a child should do better than they, made much steadier hands. This pleased Mr. Ed, and he teased them for letting little Sammy outdo them.

Delilah kept closer than ever to her son since his return, closer in a frightened, pitiful way, as if her presence would keep him safe for her, as if she must make up for what she had allowed to happen to him. But still, often whole days went by without her seeing him, for he was in the fields now with the other hands, doing work that the womenfolks could have no part in. And he seemed to have more interest outside his Maw. He talked and laughed with his companions. He seemed an important part of them, for they teased him cruelly, calling him "Dad" for his patient, old ways, and laughing uproariously at his stupid talk. But Sammy's warped mind saw such attention in a rosy light. He grinned foolishly at his nickname and cackled with the others at his own talking.

It hurt Delilah that he should love so much to be with them, that she was no longer the only comfort to his stupidity. She was in many ways more miserable since his return than she had been when he left her. It seemed impossible for her to overcome the listless, frightened misery that had become so much a part of her these last months. She was more than ever complaining that spring. The misery held her back fast all April and lasted far into May. She often refused to go into the field, and forced to do the weekly washing, she did it more dreadfully than ever. She complained of hot and cold spells running over her body and would come into the garden on the hottest days in an old sweater. She rolled her eyes in fear of Mr. Ed, but towards Old Miss she grew more and more unbearably impudent. Not even the fairness of Hannah could soothe her growing bitterness. When Mr. Ed saw fit to give her a talking, her stubbornness broke with the most unexpected and terrible deluge of tears. Mr. Ed's surprise rendered him speechless in the middle of his discipline. She refused to tell him her troubles, and promised vehemently to do better, praying all the while for her soul, her son's, and her master's so confusedly that she seemed almost mentally ill. Delilah was truly sick that spring; frightened, and unable to explain her fear.

Summer slid into being,—a black man's paradise of a summer—long, gay days; constant cooling rains until July; work and sweat and horseflies from early dawn until long after sunset; the noonday meal or a thick lunch for those who worked across the creek; the frogs' chorus at night heard at a distance from the cool, dark depth of the pond; the shrilling katydids; lightning bugs and bats; a rooster's hot crow; the sherry-sweet smell of a hay load; mosquitoes, and life standing breathless, yet days coming and ending.

A midsummer of heat prolonged itself. Delilah

wandered up and down the curving rows of cotton flopping poisoned molasses on the big wilted leaves to kill the boll weevils. Occasionally she would straighten and look far over the drooping fields to the little dot in the watermelon patch that was Sammy stringing against the crows. She sighed often and deeply but kept on at her sorry labor. Words passed among her fellow laborers, and light laughter. The sun mounted slowly, almost imperceptibly. The wind blew hot over the fields, and as the morning wore away hunger prevailed.

Little Sammy walked back and forth across the vines, working the string over the patch in a wonderful design.

He was cool and dry. He felt the blistering sun as a far away thing, but the noon glare weighed heavily upon him. His head felt wobbly, and he began to cry in his silent, painful way, walking in and out among the melons, unwinding the huge ball of wrapping string and squeezing it between the split ends of sticks that he had stuck up earlier in the vines. His side ached as he breathed, but somehow he grew accustomed to its aching; and though he wept, he did not weep so much for pain as from a hidden desire for tears at that moment. It was as if his tears would always remain unshed no matter how many he forced between his narrow puffed eyelids. The earth spun like a thousand tops around him. He sat down hard on a young, crow-picked watermelon that squashed all over his bottom and scattered gnats from its souring sweetness.

Delilah, stopping again at her work to gaze at her son, saw him sitting there. She dropped her poisoning paddle and waddled fast across the cotton, crushing the stalks with her weight.

"Blessed Jesus, whut ails my son?"

By the time she reached the lower fields and the melon patch, little Sammy's tears were all gone, only salty traces were left on his dark cheeks. He sat in the juicy sand playing with his toes, threading them with string and grinning at the tickling results. Perhaps in bending over, the pain had stopped; perhaps it was still there but grown accustomed to like tied on, broken-down shoes.

Mr. Ed, coming later, was told by his grinning but somehow sympathetic hands how little Sammy had sat in the middle of the field half the morning and would not work for any of them. The farmer sent his little hand home in the wagon, but Delilah he refused to let leave the fields.

"Sumpin' ails him bad, Mr. Ed," she pleaded. "I knows sumpin' wrong. Seem like all summer sumpin' been aimin' on happenin'."

But Mr. Ed, looking back over the summer, saw Sammy's gayety, and looking now at the boy, saw only a black, empty face with helpless eyes. Delilah alone saw the suffering there, and Hannah, too, said little Sammy was bad sick.

"He ain't got sense 'nuff to know when he hurtin' and when he ain't."

But little Sammy went home alone. Left in the cool, smelly cabin, he began cooking his Maw's dinner. When Delilah came home at noon after a wasted morning, she found the kettle boiling over, the table set, and little Sammy senseless on the floor.

TWELVE

Miz hannah came over one night to see how little Sammy did. She had seen many of her race lie down quietly and die. She sensed their weakness. Some part of Sammy's patient pain lay near her heart. She thought of his miserable life, his fear and wonder of it. She had long learned to accept her God's ways; but her soul, lying deep within her, broke with the pitifulness of Delilah's son.

The cabin spread before Hannah in the still, white moonlight. Through the window and open door pale light came out diagonally, wavering and weak in the moon glare. Inside the fire burned hot in its shell of charred rags, making the room more uncomfortable than the mosquitoes it sought to destroy. They clung around the ceiling, buzzing and half drunk with the burned, scorched smell. The ashy bricks were hot too, as the endless July night was hot. Life clung here, and death, and all the race's acceptance of them both.

The huddled rooms were still and hotly dark. Hannah called as she entered, and Delilah answered from the left room.

"Miz Hannah," she asked wearily, "is dat you?"

Hannah came in and went first to the iron bed where Sammy lay, sprawled and restless with fever. She looked down at him silently and then turned to Delilah.

"He ain't no better—" It was hardly a question for already it was answered. Delilah said nothing nor did she once stop in the monotonous fanning of her child. The Sunday School Magazine caught hesitantly at the vacant air, and the flapping noise it made going back and forth was the only sound in the huge night, save that of the crickets and katydids, promising an early frost.

After a while Hannah sighed and turned from the bed. "The doctor come?" she asked.

"Yeah."

"Whut he say?"

"He don't know nothin'."

"Whut he say?"

"I don't know whut he say. I—I—." Delilah stumbled with her words, trying to remember. "I—I—don't know." She hesitated. "He lef' some pills to give him."

"He got to leave sumpin'," Hannah scoffed resignedly. "Dey do any good?"

"I ain't give him none."

"You might's well. Dey might help; dey won't hurt."

"Dey won't do no good."

Hannah sat down then near the door.

"I 'spects you right," she said. "I doubt dey would do none."

Sammy stirred and moaned, waking from a feverish sleep.

"Maw," he called, loud and frightened at reality, "Maw."

Delilah rose and bent over him, still fanning.

"I's here, Son," she said.

"Maw, Maw, you ain't leavin' me?"

"No, Son, I's here. I ain't leavin' you."

Sammy's eyes rolled a little, wandering over the room. He turned his head from side to side.

"Maw, Maw, Maw." Delilah tried to silence his fretfulness, but he seemed unable to tell his pain and repeated the words over and over, "Maw, Maw."

He caught her hand, and Hannah came over and took the paper from Delilah and fanned for her. Sammy stared at her unseeing, while Delilah rubbed his hands and arms.

"Whut ails you, son? Whut ails my boy?"

Sammy's call went on insanely until it seemed impossible that the world could hold more of the words. But they went on until Sammy wore himself out with his tossing and drifted into a quieter sleep.

Delilah took up her fanning, and after Hannah had

stirred the fire, she, too, returned as she had been to her chair.

It was a night like a thousand summer nights. The moon rising slowly, slowly set. Hannah rose once to trim the feeble light to brave the new darkness. The Big Ben ticked, laboriously dragging the long night on. Sammy slept deeply, his body damp and hot. Occasionally the two women slept, waking easily when the child stirred. A train went by far away in the woodlands, its whistle another noise of the night. Once some dogs barked in the yard of one of the cabins, bringing after them a silence more deathly than before.

At last the sounds of the hands going to the fields, the trace chains jangling, the stomp of the mules, the low laughter, broke the stifling quiet of the night. The light, already so weak from the lamp, sputtered and went out. Soon after, the sun shot gloriously through the shutter chinks and, falling on little Sammy, woke him.

He saw Delilah bending over him, drowsy with watching. He drew his hand from her lap. She opened her eyes wide. Sammy pulled the cover high up to his nose and grinned at her. He looked devilish and hideous.

"Is you my Maw?" he asked glibly.

She thought he wandered in his words.

"Yeah, Son, I's yo' Maw. I ain't goin' leave you. No, Son."

Hannah got up from her place. She came and stood on the other side of the bed, shutting out the light that came gayly through the shutter.

Sammy plucked at his Maw's dress.

"Make her move, Maw. Make her move." He faltered. "Seem lack she shuttin' out de day."

Hannah moved to the foot of the bed. She held on to its iron curlings and turned her head toward the window. She did not cry at all.

Sammy lay still but not satisfied.

"The sun done set, Maw? It gettin' dark, ain't it?"

"No, Son, de sun ain't set. It bright day, chile, de sun just riz."

He dozed for a while, and Hannah took up the pan from the chair at Delilah's side and went into the kitchen. She emptied it of its feverish water and went to the well to draw more, cool and fresh, to bathe the child. When she returned, little Sammy lay so still with opened eyes that Hannah thought for an instant that he had died. But he turned to his Maw, and his eyes were very sane and clear. He reached for Delilah's hand. She stopped her fanning and stared at him and trembled.

"Maw." The voice was warm and steady. "Is it Friday?"

"Yeah, Son, it Friday."

"Is de mornin' train run yit?"

Delilah turned her head and sobbed.

Hannah answered. "No, Son, it ain't but nine o'clock."

Sammy did not take his eyes from his Maw. He tugged gently at her hand and patted it.

"Don't cry, Maw. It ain't for you to cry."

Hannah looked hard at him. "Oh, Lawd God," she whispered astonished.

"It sort of dark now, Maw." Sammy said, smiling in the sunshine, "It purty, Maw."

The Big Ben stumbled in its ticking, and Sammy woke from his earthly dreaming. Hannah alone heard the nine fifteen train singing down its rails two miles away and thundering across the river trestle. Delilah was staring at her little son who was dead, her eyes enormous and afraid. The third day after, Sammy was buried. The funeral was not very big. The preacher was very sincere.

"Of course," he mumbled over the casket scattered with withering summer flowers, "we all knows he ain't had much sense, (Amen, Brother), but it seems like dat now it don't matter much. Dat de Lawd knows best. But dat little black boy knew his place on earth, and when he hear de Lawd callin' 'Son!' he knowed it was time to go. He went cheerful. He'll be a missin' chile. (That's right, brother, a missin' chile.)"

Delilah sat straight and untearful through the service. She sat straight and untearful as the mourners filed by the casket and waved Sammy's soul goodbye. Then it was her time to go up for the last unreal, inadequate look. Hannah was waiting for her at the back of the church, and all the people stood silent in the yard and waited. Delilah stood and looked and looked; then she turned and looked upward, beyond the pulpit where Sammy's soul was waiting for his Maw's farewell. But she could not wave. She hid her face in her round soft hands and wept.

Alone in her cabin that night, she held her hands tight in her lap and swayed to and fro in her grief.

"Oh, Lawd," she prayed, "I ain't a good nigger, I knows dat. But I ain't had nothin' ever but my lil' boy. I wuz good to him, Lawd, I swear I wuz. Why'd you take him? Cream don't matter now, I ain't never had Cream. But Sammy war'nt nobody's but mine. Why'd you take him, Gawd, from dis po' nigger? He won't be no good in heav'n wid out his Maw. Oh, Jesus, help me!"

After a long while she grew quiet and lay in the moonlight across her bed. Over in the corner little Sammy's bed stood. Delilah turned her torn face away from its emptiness and wept silently with her face to the wall. All night long she lay still and alone. When morning came, she rose and left the cabin, and no one saw her for several days.

THIRTEEN

Without little Sammy Delilah withdrew more than ever into herself. The busy season was over, the crops laid by, so there was no need to go into the fields or any cause that she should be among others of her race. She stayed away from the Big House, too, did not even go to do the washing, and Old Miss did not send for her. Perhaps it was she had no one to send. Only occasionally did Delilah go to Hannah's for necessities, and then her visits were short and abrupt, and Hannah's sympathy was as of old, the silent kind.

So it was that no one ever saw Delilah, not even on Saturdays which used to be the one day she really let herself go. But the Negroes talked of her among themselves, and they heard too that Mr. Ed would let her go that winter because it was Sammy, alone, who had been worthy of his wages. Delilah knew, if she thought of it, that she would have to leave. Mr. Ed even went himself to her cabin when she did not come a second washday and told her that unless she were willing to do the work required of her, she would have to go. Delilah had said she would do better, but the next week, she failed again to do the washing.

Old Miss came down to give her a talking. It was during dog days—late in August. For days now it had rained sullenly. Cool, thudding rain, silent and persistent on the cabin roofs, dripping wet and dark from the trees. Old Miss, bundled in old woolens, came on foot, slushing down the muddy road. The river was reported rising, and unless the rain let up, all the corn would be lost—the second loss in three years. Delilah's was lowest in the bottoms, the heaviest headed and most mature. It was corn that Sammy had planted in love in the spring and tended in faith and hope during the summer. It was the last tangible proof, except the memories of a fainting heart, that Sammy had had his being. The rain was very monotonous, and the earth very dull that day, so that Old Miss's heart was somewhat softened for the lonely, miserable Delilah. She had come in anger, but the cabin in the mists looked so stripped of all warmth or beauty, and the poignant memory of Sammy seemed to hover so close, that she felt little anger as she climbed the stoop to the front door; instead, only an aching wonder filled her at the pain of such a life. Oh, it was impossible to know God's will with these people or her duty toward them.

"Delilah," she said gently, entering the glow and dimness from the cabin hearth and seeing the Negress sitting there alone and stooped before the fire watching her corn bread cooking among the coals, "I just came to see how you're getting along. The river's rising, you know, and all the corn will be lost."

Delilah rose and got another chair for herself, and when Old Miss was seated, she sat opposite her, silent and unmoved.

"And Delilah, why haven't you come to wash? You don't have little Sammy to do for you anymore. You must work. You can't expect Mr. Ed to keep you on and feed you for nothing. He can't do it. And if your corn goes, Delilah, what will you eat?"

"I guess de Lawd knows whut He's doin' takin' dat corn."

"But Delilah, you've got to work harder than ever without it. You can't just sit."

"If we ain't got it, we ain't got it, I say. De Lawd gives to some, and to some He don't, and it ain't our bizness, and it ain't nothin' you can do to change it. He took Sammy, didn't He? And He kin make dat river git de corn, and you can't say no more'n I kin."

The other woman was silent at the mention of Sammy's name. Who was she to preach, here in this cabin which had known a greater despair than she probably had ever dreamed of? But Delilah, sitting warm before a fire furnished through Mr. Ed's efforts, in a cabin recently mended at his own orders—sitting there, sullen and impudent—exasperated her beyond words almost, and the anger rose again in her throat.

"But Delilah, whom do you expect to feed you? Sammy's dying will make things harder than ever for you. You can't live without working. We all must do it, I as well as you. You could have a good home here with me. I need help with the garden and washing. We need to work together and help each other."

Delilah sat still in her chair. "Help each other!" she mumbled. "Help each other! Fo' de Lawd, I ain't askin' nobody to help me but myself."

Old Miss got up. She was furious. "Very well, Delilah, you can work it out yourself. Maybe you are right. We never could understand each other, and I don't suppose we ever will. I just hope you get a place that will suit you, though I don't see where it would be. I have a winter coat you could use, maybe, and if you want it, you can come and get it."

She left, and Delilah sat on in the growing darkness. The fire died down, and the room grew chill, but she sat on, stooped and still in the bowed old chair.

She sat on, thinking of her son, and her God, and her life here on the earth. It did not matter that the corn was going. That was God's will, as it had been His will to take her son and her love. Intangible things that had no apparent cause she laid to God's will. She accepted them, not without bitterness, but

with a humility growing from her awful fear of her
Maker, her Maker that had birthed her black with a
black woman's lot, that had taken from her the child
He had made unlovely to all others. She knew Him
as all powerful, vengeful in the face of wrong and
unmerciful in judgment. She was forced to accept
His will. But that of the other power in her life, the
white race, she was not forced to accept. Therefore,
she flung out to it double hate and double rebellion.
It was not unquestionable, not a shadowy, all-seeing,
all-knowing spirit, full of wind and deep long summer
days, but a living thing such as herself; and she knew
it as sinful and weak as herself. Yet, no better than
herself, that race saw fit to control Delilah's existence.
It said, do this, and do that, and because Delilah saw
herself as low and wretched with no integrity of her
own, she had done this and done that. But now she
was unafraid, with no beauty left her in life to lose.
And, almost to redeem herself for that old ungracious
obedience, she girded herself in hate and rebellion
and wrapped it hot about her. No longer need she
tramp wearily back and forth doing the will of others.
She stood in her own soul, strong in her hate.

So Delilah sat on still before her dying fire and
settled her account with God and man. The winter
lay before her, unknown; but she never thought
about its emptiness. She saw only her past, her gay,
loud youth—her child, that in the coming had meant

little or nothing to her, but in the leaving and going had meant her soul. She felt the hot path of liquor cutting down her throat. She saw her husband's face, cruel and mocking. She had grown to hate it with a hate as hot as that she flung to the white race because he, too, had demanded of her in the past, and stupidly she had obeyed. He was included in that symbol of all the ugliness and evil of her life. She had loved him once and he had betrayed that love so that it lay cold and revengeful within her. She remembered the day he had come and taken Sammy. She remembered terribly her own wretched part in that taking. She thought of the lonely days of those months Sammy was away and the mysterious vague night of his return. And above all, transcending all other memories, was that of her son's death.

When Sammy had died she had humbled herself before God, blamed her own sinfulness entirely. But now the weeks passing and the violence of her thoughts confusing her mental grasp, she blamed more her husband's part. No one knew why Sammy had died, but Delilah had wondered at his life away from her. He had left in health and returned in sickness to die. And her husband had given no account and her son none whatsoever. But he had died, and Cream had been with him during the beginning of that dying. Cream had known, yet had kept Sammy on to die.

She saw it all clearly, worn and beaten Delilah. There was no longer any place left her in the world, not even many people to remember that once there had been a Delilah. Perhaps, she thought suddenly, there was never any place for me. Perhaps I've never been—me nor Sammy, nor anyone living. No time, no nothing, just emptiness.

"Oh, Lawd Jesus!"

When her bewildered mind turned and came out to this awful void, Delilah had an acute and dreadful feeling that she was ceasing to exist and drifting out into a most terrible and unknown blackness. Frantically, she prayed, shutting her eyes tight that she might not see herself slip out and beyond and be no more. "Help me. Oh, Gawd, help me, help me."

At last her whirling brain stilled, and she opened her eyes to her dead fire and saw in its crumpled glow her husband Cream.

FOURTEEN

◆

THERE was something almost humble in the way Cream stood before Delilah shutting off the fire's glow so that he was in her eyes a sort of melting silhouette, dim and leaning toward her. He made a helpless gesture, spreading out both hands and shrugging slightly.

"Delilah," he said softly, "I done heard 'bout Sammy." He paused, wet his lips noisily and went on. "I knows how you missin' him. I sorta misses him myself." He looked miserably around the room that had once held Sammy's life and then looked back at his wife.

She sat in her chair, her hands clutched in her lap, her body taut.

Floundering, Cream went on. "I done knows how you feels. I feels dat way too. He such a pit'ful chile, and 'pears like he better'n mos' folks. Maybe 'cause he ain't had sense 'nuff, but 'pears like he ain't had no meanness in him." Cream faltered. Delilah remained quiet. "I knows how you feels," he added lamely.

The old rage seethed in Delilah, a rage that forgot all past fears. The same rage she had felt when Old

Miss offered sympathy, placing them together in the world as if their problems were the same. "We should work together, Delilah, and help each other." And now Cream, repeating humbly, "I knows how you feels."

"You killed him," she said.

Cream was startled. He stepped sideways from Delilah and the fire.

"No, Delilah, no," he whined. "We wuz good to Sammy. We never crossed him. We never thought nothin' wuz de matter 'til he run away. We never did nothin'. We—"

"We!" Delilah screamed. "You and who?" She bent and grabbed the frying pan so quickly that the handle turned in her hand and flipped out the corn bread, skidding it across the hearth. She rose and stepped toward her husband. "You and who? Whut low-down nigger gal you 'low tech my chile?" She grabbed him, her fat fingers strong and demanding. "Who'd you let kill my son?" Her voice was high but none the less potent and not to be parried.

Cream squirmed and pulled away and fought at her. "Lizzie," he stuttered, so frightened his jaw would not function. "I thought you knowed dat Lizzie keep house for me."

Delilah roared at the name. "You kill 'im," she screeched. "You bof' done kill 'im!"

She swung the frying pan in a wide arc. Cream

stepped back but stumbled over Delilah's chair. As he regained his balance, the pan's iron rim caught at his temple and ripped through his face. He crumpled weakly and lay jerking spasmodically on the floor. Then he was still.

Delilah looked down on her murdered husband. Not for several seconds did she notice the frying pan still in her hand, the edge of it bloody and rimmed with flesh. She sat down then and laid it stupidly but neatly beside her. She whimpered slightly, and began to stroke the sole of Cream's shining shoe. Not until hours later, when she saw the car, did she grow afraid.

FIFTEEN

———◆———

IN THE rain and wind Miss Minnie's younguns played on the road. With the old battered wagon, surviving last Santa Claus, they clattered down the hill to Miz Hannah's, one standing up and guiding while another stuck on raggedly behind and a third sat on the lumber pile on the hilltop and minded Baby Ruth. Their legs were skinny and tireless; their hearts close to nature and unhampered. They fussed and played, and the whole of God's world was theirs.

When Cream drove up to Miz 'Lilah's in his long, blue car, they stopped playing and stood together beside the lumber and watched this black god. They were silent then, but with Cream good in the house, they clamored like sea gulls with fresh prey.

"He think he sumpin'," Will said.

"He tink he sumpin'," Young Joe's echo was like a little weak tune played on a comb.

"He think he sumpin', ridin' up in a fine otomobile and sass'n' 'round like he own Heav'n. He don't tho', he sho' don't," and the black face grinned at the blue car. "And he ain't even goin' dere. He ain't ever goin' dere. He goin' jus' de op'site. He goin' to Hell—l—l-l." Will held the last word until it was a high wail in the cool air.

"He goin' to Hell-l-l!" the younger ones took up the chant and danced round and round with it. "He goin' to hell. Mr. Cream goin' to Hell, to Hell—l!" Maggie was holding the baby and soon grew tired of this dance, and was provoked when she realized that she was the one burdened at such a time.

"Shet yo' mouf!" she hissed, slapping the unsuspecting Will. "Shet yo' mouf. Don't you know it a sin to say Hell?"

A pall came upon them in their gayety. They looked solemnly at the irate Maggie whose lips trembled suddenly as she sat down on the lumber.

"Maw done tol' you it a sin to say Hell, and dat somebody goin' dere. Ain't nobody knowin' where none of us is goin'. And Mr. Cream, jus' 'cause he rich ain't sayin' he got to be damned to brimstone and fire. Not 'cause he rich and ride in a long car, it ain't."

"Yeah, but Jesus say in de Bible," Will said, gathering momentum for his defense, "in de Bible, Jesus say it easier for de rich man to go through de eye of a sewing needle dan it is for him to enter de Kingdom of Heav'n. Dat meant he can't go to Heav'n a tall, 'cause you know he can't go through no needle."

"When de Bible say 'needle,'" Maggie said in a voice of great strength and wisdom, "it ain't meanin' reg'lar needles like we has. It meanin' sumpin' diff'unt. When de Lawd speaks 'bout things dey ain't never reg'lar, 'cause all things is poss'ble in de eye of de Lawd. He kin stretch an old needle whichever way it's needin' to go, or He could shrink a man up whichever ways and git 'im through anything needful. Dat's de way de Bible say."

She said it so emphatically that all grounds for disagreements melted and flowed away beneath them. The children stood ringed around her, wide-eyed, convinced and wordless. Only Will was unimpressed. He had not been listening even, not since Maggie had said, "Jus' 'cause he rich ain't saying he got to be damned."

"Jus' 'cause he rich," Will thought. Minnie's years of admonishing vanished from his mind. The hard-taught dignity of his rags and penniless state became unreasonable. A huge relief and joy filled his heart and made him almost tired. All of his life, since he could remember, since Mr. Cream had come for Sammy in the long, blue car, Will had wanted to own such an automobile, had wanted to be just as slick and as rich as Mr. Cream. But he had scorned it in his mind and held himself above; now, Maggie, herself, put de Lawd's stamp on it. "Someday," Will thought, "I's gonna be rich, too, and own me a fine, blue car and wear slicked-up clothes. And I's gonna ride all over de country, and folks will look at me with wantin' in dere hearts and say, 'Dere go Will Foster. He think he sumpin' ridin' in dat fine, blue car.' "

Then it seemed that Cream's car was his, and he walked over to it, swaggering carefully in Cream's way.

"Dis here my car," he said. "I's gonna take a ride."

Maggie came to herself as he opened the door. She clutched the baby and rushed forward.

"No, you ain't," she screamed, catching at her brother's arm. "No you ain't, you crazy fool nigger. Dat ain't yo' car, and you ain't goin' on no ride. You ain't got no mo' sense dan a guinea hen potranking in de rain, sayin' she done laid an aigg when she ain't."

Will tried to push her away and shut the door. Maggie, holding onto the baby, beat at him with little restraint. A flying fist soon struck the youngest, and she began to cry deafeningly.

Young Joe pulled at Maggie's skirts nervously. "Mr. Cream, Mr. Cream'll be comin' out here."

Maggie jerked back and whirled toward the cabin. Delilah stood in her half-opened door looking out at them. She said nothing at all, just looked through the growing darkness, the whites of her eyes glowing in the wet twilight, and the green of them palely flashing.

Maggie flew away with Young Joe and Baby

Ruth, leaving where they had stood a vacant rush of air. Will slunk low beneath the wheel, his eyes frozen to Delilah's, his lips sullen and pouting.

But raging words never came from Delilah. She never moved but stood looking at the car, unable to take her eyes from the dimming, vague shape of it. After a long while, she shut the door.

SIXTEEN

UNTIL the screaming of Baby Ruth stirred Delilah from her cramped stooping by Cream's side, she had had no realization of the thing she had done. She had murdered her husband; there were laws about murder. Yet, until that moment when Delilah looked through her door at the blue shadow below the ditch-bank, until she saw that car that had been so much a part of her husband's living, she had not been afraid at all for herself. She had had no feeling beyond a loneliness and a sort of vacancy. But now, after shutting the door on the blue car low lying on the road, hoping to shut out from her mind, as well, the reality of it, a desperate, strangling fear flooded her. She struggled with it for a long, long while, there leaning against the door, facing the room where Cream lay in his own blood.

Darkness crept through the shutters and cracks and settled firmly into the corners of the room. The fire had long ago died, and a heavy chill and damp-ness lay everywhere. It was this coldness that first brought Delilah to life, and after she had rebuilt the fire so that its cheerfulness flickered over the room, she was no longer congealed by her fear. Instead, it forced her into a steady action, and she did all those things she had to do with swift and definite ease. It wasn't much later than midnight when she knocked at the side door of the Big House. She knocked loudly, and it was not necessary to ring the bell before Mr. Ed came to the door in his nightshirt.

"Delilah?" he asked sleepily, and then seeing her face. "Good Lord, woman, what's wrong?"

"Mr. Ed, Mr. Ed," and suddenly she was crying as she always cried before this man who of all others seemed strong enough and deep enough and kind enough to understand her soul.

He looked at her a moment, a hard, questioning look. "Come in here, Delilah, come on in the back room."

He led the way and sat her down on one of the small cane chairs. He left her there alone for a while and went back to his own room to dress more fully. Through her tears Delilah could hear Old Miss ask who it was and what was wrong. The answer was low and indistinguishable. Old Miss did not come back with her husband.

"Well, Delilah, what is it?"

"I killed Cream, Mr. Ed."

"You killed him?"

"Yassuh, I done killed him."

"Did he hurt you?"

"No, suh, Mr. Ed. He never teched me."

"What made you kill him, Delilah?"

"I don' know, Mr. Ed. I don' know."

She was no longer crying. She was calm now and felt almost safe.

"He come 'bout Sammy, and we wuz talkin', and when he said dat gal been wid him, I thought maybe dey killed Sammy. It looked dat way den. And I killed him. I never knowed I'd git to killin' him, but I done it."

"What gal was with him?"

"Not den, Mr. Ed. No gal wuz wid him den. He come by hisself 'bout Sammy. But she been wid him in Winston. She wid him when he took Sammy. She keep house fer him."

Mr. Ed was silent for awhile. Delilah sat still, looking at the floor.

"So," the man said, "you've killed Cream. It was the wrong way out, Delilah, but you've done it now. What are you going to do? The coroner will have to come over. You'll have to go to court, Delilah. You might get out on self defense. We'll have to see. They can make it hard for you."

"Yassuh, Mr. Ed."

"Go on home tonight. Leave Cream however he is. Maybe you could stay with Hannah. Try to get some sleep."

Delilah sat with her eyes still on the floor. She

did not raise them for a long time. When she did look at her master, there was something in them lost and humbled, something questioning and haunted.

"Cream ain't dere, Mr. Ed."

"He ain't there? Where is he then? You killed him there, didn't you?"

"Yassuh, Mr. Ed. I kill him dere fo' de fireplace wid de skillet. But he ain't dere now."

"Where is he, Delilah?"

"I burrit Cream, Mr. Ed."

"You—what?"

"I burrit Cream," Delilah went on slowly with extreme care. "After I seen de car, I knowed whut I had to do. I washed all de blud up 'round de flo', and I bathed Cream real good. I brushed his clothes and wiped de mud off'n his shoes, and den I waited 'till good dark and come down here and got me a shovel and a wheel barrel. Den I dug a hole down in de holler, and after dat, I went and got Cream. I roll him on de wheel barrel, and I burries him."

"What the devil made you do that. All this rain—."

"I'd killed, Mr. Ed, and niggers dat kill ain't got much chance. And de car settin' out dere skeared me. Dat look like Cream wuz dere, and I never wants Cream to be dere. Dat wouldn't do fer dem to find him dere."

"Cream's car is there? You should never have moved Cream then, Delilah. If the car's there, then

Cream should be there in some form. You shouldn't have buried Cream, Delilah. It looks bad for you."

"It all right, Mr. Ed. It all right. All you gotta do is move dat car. You jus' take it off down de road den nobody'll know de car been dere. Dat all you needin' to do, Mr. Ed. I done done all de rest. You jus' take it off down de road, and nobody'll know whut I done to Cream."

"But maybe someone saw Cream come, Delilah. He came this afternoon, didn't he?"

"No, suh, Mr. Ed? No suh. It after dark when Cream come. Long time after dark. Dey'll hardly know 'bout it after dark."

Delilah was growing afraid again. They did know that Cream had come. She remembered the frightened faces of Minnie's children turned up to her, and Will petulant and withdrawn beneath the steering wheel. She was growing afraid again—afraid that Mr. Ed would not drive the car away, afraid very much of the power of this man, so afraid that she lied knowing that he knew she lied, but somehow that lie pushed back her fear and held it dammed and it could not flood her heart and panic it as it had done that time when she shut the cabin door on the blue car.

For a long while Mr. Ed asked no question nor talked at all. And Delilah sat straight and still and a little angry, pressing back her fear with that anger and the lie that brought it forth.

Then Mr. Ed got up. He said softly, "Go on home, Delilah. Go on home to bed, Forget about the car. It'll be all right. Everything will be all right. Just don't talk, Delilah. Hear, Delilah? Just don't talk."

"No, suh, Mr. Ed. No, suh."

It was all right again. Mr. Ed knew it was all right. Mr. Ed would never let them get her. She got up awkwardly and very slowly stumbled to the door he held open for her. She went through it and hesitated, then turned her green eyes toward the man behind her. There was a liquid, soft quality to them, a humbleness and gratefulness and awe mixed together.

"You been good to me." She said. "I ain't fergettin', you been good to me."

SEVENTEEN

W H E N Delilah opened her door on the early dawn of a new day and looked out at the road, the blue car was no longer there. There were no signs either of tracks in any direction—only gravel and mud and a thick wetness. Across the road beyond the rye field Hannah's house snuggled against the earth of the hill, and down to the left the Big House showed drearily damp but somehow secure and solid. It was very early yet, and there were no sounds in the Sunday morning save the quickening dampness of the wind and rain. The world lay sluggish as if it were sullen and unwilling to waken.

Delilah closed the door and went back into her kitchen. She felt as the earth had looked—miserably half asleep yet fearing to face alertness. Nothing seemed real any more, nothing but the nothingness itself. She knew that she must never feel again or think or remember, never have anything at all but nothingness. In that way she might live on.

She did not leave the cabin at all that day, and no one came until almost dark. Hannah came then, inviting herself in, full of her day and her children's visits. The preacher and visiting reverend had had dinner with her, and her oldest daughters and their husbands had come over to be with their Maw. Hannah said it had been as nice a day as anyone could have had.

Delilah sat quietly, clutching at her nothingness.

"Miss Minnie's chaps come over affer dinner," Hannah went on, "and dey say dat Cream of yourn was here yes'tiddy."

Delilah started, not visibly, but she felt her heart leap for a moment before she could still it.

"I ain't got nothin' to do wid dat Cream," she said.

"Look like he got sumpin' to do wid you." Hannah made no pretense of keeping the curiosity from her voice and eyes.

Delilah sat in her chair with her hands folded in her lap. There was little hint of what was going on within her. Hannah's eyes glistened toward her. She half grinned.

"Whut Cream here for, Miz 'Lilah?"

"I ain't say Cream been here."

"Dem chaps ain't seein' his ghost."

Delilah jerked. She rolled her eyes about the room and wet her lips.

"I ain't knowin' whut dem chaps see."

"I don't know whut all you got to be so secrety 'bout. He been here, and now he done left. Whut he comin' here for now?"

Delilah relaxed her hands.

"Yeah," she said, "he done been here, and now he done lef'. He ain't wantin' nothin'. He jus' ask 'bout Sammy."

"Dat a man for you," Hannah scoffed. "He got nerve askin' 'bout Sammy. Don't he know 'bout Sammy?"

"He know," Delilah said.

"Whut you tell him? Whut you say?"

"Nothin'. I ain't say nothin', and he jus' lef' after a while, and I never done nothin'."

"Warn't nothin' you could do," Hannah said, her curiosity appeased. "But it would've been mighty sat'fying if you had killed him."

Delilah sat stiller than at any time the whole afternoon. She said nothing at first. A sudden wind blew against the shutters and came down the chimney, sending out a puff of ashes and filling the room with a sweet pine smoke smell. A whistle of rain came with it and beat mournfully over the cabin.

"It gittin' darker." Delilah said, "And startin' to rain again. Maybe you better go, Miz Hannah, fo' it gits any worse."

Hannah looked at her friend surprised. Then she got up slowly.

"Sammy gone," she said. "Ain't right for you to think on whut's been. De past is gone 'cordin' to de Lawd's will. It's best forgot 'bout. If Cream, he's sorry, and you is wantin' him back, forgit whut he done. A woman needs a man when she gits older; and after he old too, things is most likely to be diff'unt. It just ain't right you livin' shut up days by yo' self. It ain't right, Miz 'Lilah."

Delilah turned her head to hide the tears that came at this strange unexpected sympathy at such an ironical time. ·

"Dey's a lot in dis world dat ain't right."

Hannah only shook her head. "It's yo' life," she said, "and yo' bizness. I ain't meddling none, I's jus' tellin' you."

With that, she left the cabin.

EIGHTEEN

It was early on Tuesday that Pignine woke his Maw. She lay in the shadowed light of the young morning, looking at her son with absorption, hearing the rain on the tin roof, letting her senses have all the time they needed to come together from their sleep. Then she turned her head on the pillow and said drowsily, "Whut wrong now?"

She knew all the time that there was something really wrong. She had sensed, too, that it would be one of those things there was no doing anything about; so she lay in the morning light quietly, acquainting her mind and her body gently with this new thing.

"Whut wrong now?" she asked in her own good time.

Pignine shut the door behind him and came softly to his Maw's bed. He stood before her, seeming big in the tiny low-ceilinged room. His hands were hanging loosely at his side, and sometimes in his talking he brought them together for a moment.

"Maw," he said. His voice was low and gently

mumbled as if his words were padded somehow by the dimness. "Dey is affer Miz 'Lilah."

Hannah pulled up the flour-sack sheets to her throat and crossed her arms over them.

"Whut dey know?" she asked.

"Dey say she know where Mr. Cream is. Dey say she—" Pignine wet his lips. "Dey say—she know."

"Dey say she killed him?" Hannah sounded almost impatient.

"Yas'm. Lizzie done come to Miz Minnie's. She say she know Cream come here, and she ain't heared of him since. Carrie, she dere when Lizzie come. She tell me 'bout it. She say Lizzie goin' to de sheriff and dey gonna come 'rest Miz 'Lilah."

"Where Carrie?"

"She come wid me. She outside. She told me." Pignine's eyes were filled with pride at Carrie's loyalty, and they pled with Hannah to recognize it.

Hannah turned her head again.

"Yeah," she said unsmiling. "She awright. Go on out, Son. I'll be dere in a secon'."

She dressed quickly and with some pain, for always in the early morning when she rose, there seemed no will great enough to force her rebelling, weary body to movement. But she dressed fairly quickly and came out on the porch where Carrie and Pignine stood in the vague light. The slender trees about the cabin were solidly wet from the constant rain. Their early dim shadows even were wet.

"Carrie," she said, "stay here wid de chaps and see dey stay out mischief. And Pignine you go tell Mr. Ed all you know. And I'll go on over to Miz 'Lilah's, and you come dere and tell us whut he say. And you tell him everything. Don't you miss no part of nothin'."

Clinging to the post, Hannah let herself off the porch and went down the wet hill to the other cabin.

When Pignine came to them at Delilah's, they were sitting silently together in the cabin. Delilah's face looked blank and unmoved.

"Mr. Ed say come on down dere."

Hannah sat on in her chair.

"Go see whut he say, Miz 'Lilah," she said, "and den you come on back to de house. He a white man, and he know de law. You go on dere, and I'll go home and straight'n' out de chaps. Den you let us know whut he say, and we'll come over and be wid you. Dis'll be a dark time, but Mr. Ed all right. He know; and he'll make it all right."

Delilah seemed dazed, indifferent almost. She did not answer but got up and stumbled out into the slow, sad rain of the new day.

NINETEEN

◆

Delilah stood before her master once again. She felt no nervousness; she had nothing to hide or tell. There was no struggle within her, for it was done, and there was no looking back. Neither could she look forward. She would live only this minute at this time and would blot out all the great regrets and possibilities of both past and future.

Mr. Ed looked out through the white wooden columns of the side porch where the rain glazed all the yard with a crystal enamel. He wondered what her heart held.

"Things look bad, Delilah."

"Yassuh, Mr. Ed. I's a nigger."

"Yeah, a nigger that's killed her husband."

Delilah felt no hate at the sudden harshness his voice held. Her mind was grasping, holding onto, and eliminating a hundred ideas. They would glare out at her, then fade before she could catalogue the significance of any of them. She saw that it was not just her color that was wrong, that it wasn't God, or circumstances, or herself. It was hard to be a nigger because in some inexplicable way many parts of life

—harmless, maybe wonderful, in themselves—had been made bad. A million things had gone together to make a whole, and she had never known which of these things to build up and which to struggle against so that the whole would shape up differently. How dark it all was, how far from truth she had come. The bitterness was gone now, but she was helpless still. And she was very, very tired. She was a nigger who had killed her husband.

"I'll do whut you say, Mr. Ed."

The anger left his voice, and his gray eyes softened.

"There's nothing much to do. You got a slim chance however you take it. But it'll probably be a light sentence, Delilah. It wouldn't be too bad. Cream's not liked around here, but you ain't either. Some people think you are queer, and the darkies feel it same as the whites."

Delilah's eyes raised, flickered up and followed his expression closely. She was above all anger. She felt humility only—that there was still no part of it which she knew how to change.

"I knows I been wrong." She had lowered her eyes to the crack in the porch floor, but she saw nothing of it.

"You didn't know, Delilah. You can't always tell. You just shouldn't have buried Cream. It makes it look like you had so much to hide."

"I jus' done it. It looked like the thing to do, jus' to hide him away and cover it all up."

Mr. Ed's eyes narrowed and seemed to grow more intense. He could already hear his lawyer saying, "Well, Ed, I just don't see—"

"Delilah, I'm going to Lancaster to see Mr. Walters. I want you to come, too. A lawyer understands these things and will know more what we should do."

"I'll do whut you say. I'll go wherever you take me."

"Well, you go get ready to come with me. I don't want the sheriff to find you here. We need time to get this straight."

"All right, suh."

She turned to go, but he went on.

"You got anyone in Lancaster you could stay with a couple of days?"

She thought a moment, her back to him. Then she turned to answer timidly, apologetic that she was still of no help.

"No suh, I ain't been round in so long, ain't nobody dere I could go to."

"Ain't Hannah got some people there?"

"I got a sister in Rock Hill I ain't seen in a long time."

"Hannah's got some folks there, on this side of town as you go in. You go get Hannah and tell her to go with us. We'll see about things, Delilah. You just do like I say. Doing things your way hasn't done you any good, so let's try mine."

"Yassuh, you's right. I ain't meanin' to be so hard all de time."

Delilah went out between the shrubs where the late shadows sulked in the morning light. Her shoulders touched the stiff, overhanging branches of the Pyracantha. Its amber, burning berries, glistening in the dampness, shook great drops all over her like a baptismal.

"God help us all," Mr. Ed thought as he shut the door.

TWENTY

BUT Delilah did not go tell Hannah. She really meant to do everything that Mr. Ed said. But she didn't. It was raining so hard when she left the Big House that she hurried straight home. And even after she had dressed as dryly as possible for such weather, she did not go. She stood at the window and watched the rain.

It was impossible to imagine that there had ever been a sun-filled dawn. The two old oaks stood drenched, hardshelled, defiant. The road was slush, and the field beyond it that sloped to Hannah's hill gleamed redly, its terraces overflowing with water the color of its earth. The delicate green-gold grain was drowned in its one-inch height. Hannah's cabin and all the trees that stood in a little bunch around it and all the earth of the mound it sprung from were joyless and gray. To the left, barely seen from between its pecan and oak trees, the Big House opened dark, unblinking windows to the sky. Its white chimneys were without smoke in this early morning. Delilah could find no joy in the day that began for her. She looked it over carefully at this point.

Then she saw an obscure but recognizable figure come out on Hannah's porch. It was Carrie who glanced toward her, examined the weather, and went back in. Delilah felt bewildered. It wasn't that she doubted Hannah's loyalty, but seeing Carrie there had confused her mental grasp of Hannah's devotion. She had become unsure of anything at all. She had given Mr. Ed authority to act for her, and she was lost in any situation for which he had not prepared her. She turned then from her window back into her cabin and thought no more of going for her friend. She sat and waited for Mr. Ed to come.

It seemed a long time that she waited. There was nothing to do; she was dressed and waiting. And the room was cold, dark, and impregnated with dampness. The fire she and Hannah had built earlier was only coals now. Delilah added little wood to it, afraid to leave too big a fire on her hearth. Though she pulled her chair close, it still offered little cheer. Her mind was crowding with her old unhappy feelings. The past kept pushing forward. She remembered those many times she had watched a slow fire burning—with Hannah through dull evenings that seemed secure and happy now. There had been charred rags on the hearth the night Sammy died. She had been sitting just as she was now, not many days ago when Cream had come. She had nursed her loneliness and bitterness before her dimly glowing hearth until murder had grown from it. She had knelt before her weak, little fire and scrubbed up her husband's blood. Now she sat and waited for a white man to come and take her away. She could not bear much longer the four walls of her cabin closing in upon her. The past kept reaching out from their shadows and clutching and screaming at her. And she simply must not look back, nor could she look far forward, and in the present there was not one good thought to fill a second of her time.

She got up and took down her cracked patent leather pocketbook from the top shelf of the ungainly wardrobe. Then she went again to her window to watch for Mr. Ed. She wondered what she would tell him about Hannah's not coming. The rain had slackened, but the whole earth looked soaked to its marrow.

The car was starting in the garage behind the Big House. She heard it back and turn to come up the hill. It plowed forward, the tempo of its motor rising higher and higher, holding at its maximum speed as the wheels spun. Then the sound died away, and the car backed again.

Delilah's heart was plunging furiously. She had been startled when she first heard the car and realized that she would soon be leaving. But now she was keyed to a pitch of feeling she had not often experienced before. She did not want to go. She dreaded to leave; but she could not bear to stay here and wait.

The car pulled forward again, the wheels spun again, and Mr. Ed backed. Delilah knew he was stuck even before she heard him calling Pignine across the valley. She knew why she had felt so strange and lonely, why she had not tried to go for Hannah. She had known all along that this was the way it had to be—that there was only herself, and that there would never be anyone else to help her with her life. She had had it thrust upon her too often, too much, too bitterly. For a little while she had rested, someone else had been responsible and would fix it all up for her. But all along she had known—"Not for long," deep down she had been warned. There was only herself.

And she must get away from the cabin! How urgent it was that she leave! That she shut her two doors forever until that time came when they could be opened up again and the ragged dusty corners aired of all their persistent ghosts, when the warm air of happiness and gay life could blow away the morose failures that nagged at each along the walls. Until the cabin could smile again, and she could smile serenely with it, too, Delilah wanted never to come to it again to be enclosed with all those things its four walls held.

She let herself out the back door. The sound of Mr. Ed's calling Pignine came to her around the cabin, and she walked away from it toward the river. She cut through the woods and skirted Minnie's house which seemed harmless and vacant. She reached the pines that fringed the hardwoods, and they absorbed and comforted her. They smelt fresh of quiet rain mingled with the green pine oil of their needles. Unafraid they seemed, and their security lifted the feelings of urgency that had sent her out so fast. She had not planned anything, but her actions seemed to be falling in line, and something seemed to be carrying her on persistently and quietly. She reached the winding river road washed white and smooth and plastered with drab fallen leaves that were spongy underfoot. Faintly at first the flooding river's roar drew her on. It was not a new sound to her, but it was always shocking, unreal, and without a place in the usual nature of her home. It swelled and dimmed and called and coaxed her. And she moved on toward it, left the security of her woods and followed the little rutted road through cotton fields that were just opening their white harvest; but the early bolls looked wet, diseased, and untimely. Here the world grew wild again. Heavy clouds were driven rapidly across the slate sky. The wind swept freely, and the lush Means grass along the road and terraces and the trees which fringed the entire field were bowed and then tossed up stiffly. The bottom lands where the river roared were hidden from her by a heavy woodland that covered the steep slope that bordered them. She could hear the river clearly now, unbound, jubilant, immoral. She reached the brow of the hill and looked down the road which fell away between the trees and twisted its way and was lost far below in cornfields that were luxuriant with promised fruitfulness. Still the corn stood proudly, defiant of threatened disaster. But even though the wind had not reached the valley, the whole nature of it trembled and breathed fearfully. The water inched its way up.

The rain came again, and the clouds drooped low with their great weight. Delilah went down slowly, her eyes on the valley. She crossed through the trees to the spring at the bottom of the hill. Here a shallow shelter was cut, and spiders spun their webs on the walls and swung above the darkly prismatic water. Delilah knelt and cupped her hands and drank, not from thirst but habit. How many times she had sought the sweet coolness of the spring, a haven from the dusty, sun-drenched cotton furrows. But now the coolness was a dreary kind, even cold. Delilah huddled from it and felt that there would never be a sun or heat strong enough to warm her body through. She wanted desperately to sleep so deeply that she might waken buoyant and light to meet her life. But unrest rippled through her. She sat, apparently relaxed, while every nerve was on the alert, rebelling against her weariness.

So she sat huddled and awake and watched the river rising like a great swelling pain beneath her. Her eyes were dark, dark green and blank. Nothing seemed to touch her mind or soul. She saw the thick water turning on itself—in places so still and persistent, in places throbbing, unloosed. It spilled through low lands, emptied into other currents and closed around little knolls and slopes of land covering them over smooth. And in her watching it seemed to Delilah that the waters of her life were closing too, and the streams meeting one another and flowing on together into a boundless emptiness. The thought overwhelmed her. She felt strangled by it as if an eternal blankness was swooping down and engulfing her. She struggled out into the beating rain and clung to a chestnut tree by the stream and faced the wild sky and begged peace of it and sanity. After calmness came, her heart flooded her body with warm relaxing blood. Then this fearful anxiety seemed to her foolish. She straightened and carried her own weight proudly and glanced sharply at the strange world about her—the sky touching the earth, the wind blowing over the flood. She walked to the very edge of the water where it was backing and rising steadily. The corn tassels were shaking their dampness to the winds, the land seemed to give itself in sensuous gladness to the warm soft water. What had it all to do with her, or she with it? What could she be doing here wandering by a flooding river? She stood and thought calmly.

"I will go to my sister's in Rock Hill. I'll send Mr. Ed word from there. It will be all right. Mr. Ed will fix it up from there, and it will be all right."

She could cross the river by the ferry, though in all probability it had been sunk by now. That being the case she would walk the railroad trestle, a thing she had never done and had always felt incapable of. No matter, the flood would be between her and those many enemies of her life at Mr. Ed's. Afterwards she would rest and collect her wits to start the fight again.

Wagon roads cut all through the bottom lands. Any one of them would lead her down to the ferry or the few hundred yards further to the trestle. All of them were partially under water already but she knew them well for they cut lanes through twelve-foot corn. It was necessary that she hurry, too. It would be at least a mile walk, and the water grew deeper by the minute.

She took off her shoes and stockings, already soaked, and waded slowly out. The rain and wind seemed stopped now. There was silence and stillness except for the lapping movement of the water which

was warm not cold, and the sandy ground underneath was firmly packed. Delilah knew, at last, by
her own deductions where she would go. Everything was natural again and as it should be. The
events of the last few days seemed uncomplicated
and easily dealt with. She was tired—yes, and wanted
desperately to sleep. But that would come soon. Her
sister's home, known scantily at best and remembered indifferently, became a sweet place in her
mind. There, tonight, she would sleep deeply and
without fear.

A drainage ditch cut the road. It was fringed with
willow sprouts and lay low in the bottoms. As Delilah approached it, the water deepened, coming
slightly above her knees. Without the thick standing
corn on either side, it held a free course here, flowing
swift and strong. Delilah was an awkward and unbalanced figure. She held her skirts high and felt
cautiously with her feet for the bridge. It would be
only a few feet wide and without railings.

But the bridge was washed away. Delilah went
down with a slow, even plunge. There were the
broken, piled planks, slick with mud, and the willow
branches that snapped as she pulled on them. And
ribbon-like Means grass everywhere, tangling and
confusing her. At first, she was hardly afraid and almost laughed at the sly, silly way she had slipped in.
But now the river seemed enormous, and the flood

had swollen out of all proportion. It washed over her without pity; it was liquid under her weight, rushing her forward, pulling her under, smothering, dark red, invulnerable.

She fought, gasped for air, strangled. There seemed to be no coming out of it, and this was impossible, ridiculous. "I can't be drowning," she thought, and gasped again in a brief space of air. But nothing brought relief to her constricted lungs, only severe pain that seemed to swell them until they filled her entire body. Then there was an agonizing moment of complete struggle.

The fire of the water darkened. Blackness engulfed her. No more glimpses of slate, glistening sky, no whirling, tossing trees. She grew still, and her mind shut upon itself. She had never known this before. Her life was there, neither good nor bad, but her life.

"I's Delilah Massey Stewart," her mind whispered, "a Nigger woman."